Hands of Love

BY
DAVID REED

ISBN: E-Book # 978-1-966556-99-2

Paperback # 978-1-968843-00-7

Hardcover # 978-1-968843-01-4

Printed in United States of America

Cover Design by: Authors Hike

Publisher: Authors Hike

For permission requests, please contact: dreed1232@gmail.com

Acts 17:24

The God who made the world and everything in it is the Lord of heaven and earth and does not live in temples built by human hands.

1 John 4:8

Whoever does not love, does not know God, because God is love.

Hands of Love

Table of Contents

Chapter 1 – Supernatural Spirits

After 49 wonderful years of a "BEAUTIFUL" life, she was gone! My beautiful bride and soulmate was gone. She fought the battle with cancer for two and a half years. Despite her strength and resilience, she didn't survive and ultimately succumbed to her illness. She left this world on July 29, 2020, at 3:14 p.m. Needless to say, I was sad, confused, hopeless, and ready to surrender all. It was very hard to watch; one second, she was here and then in one second, she was gone.

Not after many days her demise started to take its toll on me. Half of me and all my memories were gone. I quickly hit rock bottom, as if I were tossed to the bottom of the sea. I asked God why he didn't take me, too. However, before she passed, Jeannie had said to me several times, "Remember, honey, when I am gone, life is for the living." As that thought played over and over in my mind, my whole perspective changed. It soon became clear, as if the angels were speaking to me. It made me realize that the work that God had sent me for was not over. He wanted me to share my struggles to help others get through the loss and grieving. Her words, echoing in my mind, also helped me answer the big question: Do I seek a new soulmate, or do I live life alone?

Supposedly, many of the readers of this book will be able to relate to my story. Sad to say, there comes a time in everyone's life when one soulmate departs, leaving their better half behind, grieved and dismantled. And that could be you, for death is inevitable. When it happens, you will likely find yourself in a whirlwind, just as I did, with a plethora of questions about what to do and when to do it.

Knowing that God has the whole world in his hands, including you and me, he led my spirit in the direction of a concept that I call "Hands of Love," which we will cover in several chapters of this book. However, before we move into the details, I would like to give you a brief introduction. I will begin by saying that it was something that guided me through the very uncertain times, especially when I was seeking a new soulmate for me. Though this quest was not about finding a perfect match (with Jesus being the only perfect person to live in the flesh), we know we are all a work in progress, working in our relative domains to make something good out of ourselves.

As I began writing, as well as rewriting the spiritual message that God was imparting to me, I soon discovered that the core of this non-fiction spiritual message was focusing on how deeply the "Fruits of the Spirit" should be rooted and weaved into the spirit person of my future soulmate.

The keyword here is "rooted." These qualities are human traits, universal and easily recognized by others. Although they are essential elements to the spiritual core of all Christians, they are not just meant for them. Rather, it is proximate to the entire human race, irrespective of race, color, religion, or creed. When one develops a strong relationship with God, his refined fruits of the spirit greatly increase your chances of a long and happy marriage relationship. **The key point here is that** the root of all the fruits is Love, which is God and his transformative powers.

To grasp the essence of "God's Hands of Love," one needs to first understand the power of these invisible qualities of the spirit that exist in all of us. I hope to make these qualities so clear to you that you will feel blessed and motivated to start your personal pursuit of these God-given life-changing qualities as they led me to the new soulmate that God had planned for me.

You may have been a Christian for a long time but never realized just how necessary it is to focus on your growth and develop an understanding of these fruits. Once the seeds of the fruits take root and begin to grow in your spirit you will begin to clearly see how your life will become better as it will provide you a solid foundation to choose your soulmate wisely. If you are married, it will improve your relationship with your existing soulmate, or help you to become a better person in helping others through their tough times.

It all begins with a clear understanding of how the spirit works and how the innate and invisible qualities of the spirit that we all possess communicate with God and other people.

Jesus made clear in John 4:24 (NIV): "God is spirit, and his worshipers must worship in the Spirit and in truth." Then Jesus said in John 14:6 (NIV): "Jesus answered, 'I am the way and the truth and the life. No one comes to the Father except through me.'" He adds to that advice in John 14:15-17 (NIV), assuring us that he will give us the spirit of truth: "If you love me, keep my commands. And I will ask the Father, and he will give you another Advocate, who will never leave you. He is the Holy Spirit, who leads into all truth. The world cannot receive him, because it isn't looking for him and doesn't recognize him."

God makes clear that he resides in us and gives his true followers the spirit of truth—the only truth. So, if we want truth and answers to our tough situations in life, we must seek God. Truth is, God works in our lives to help us mature in the fruits of our spirit, and consequently, they help perfect our walk with him.

He reveals himself through the special God interventions in our lives (which I call "God stories"). When you can look back and see many God stories in your life, although his communication is invisible, it becomes undeniable that God is always at work in our lives.

Let me give an example of the invisible power of the spirit. Have you ever seen a baby crying and wondered why it was crying? We usually think the baby must be hungry, or have a dirty diaper, or have some gas pains! Often, the baby is in a nursery, and one of the nursery attendants will try to help by picking it up and holding it, but the baby continues to cry.

So, at the last resort, the nursery attendant pages the mom for a meeting. As soon as the mom picks her baby up and wraps it in her arms, the baby stops crying. Magic, right? How does a baby know it is the mom? Is it her voice-maybe, her touch-maybe, her smell, or is it the invisible communication of the spirit, a very supernatural force in our likeness of God that communicates in a sphere unbeknown to the child;

that's my mom! God speaks to us or directs our thoughts through the same spirit. We don't fully understand the spiritual world, but God assures us it is very real.

We have all had moments when we met a stranger, but for some unknown reason, we felt compelled to greet that person. So, is it God's supernatural spirit speaking to our spirit? Is he leading us to that person's crying spirit to offer them his gift of love? I would say with great confidence, yes.

God speaks to us in the spirit, and he directs our steps to disperse his love to those he puts into our path daily. He clearly states in Proverbs 16:9 (NIV): "In their hearts humans plan their course, but the Lord establishes their steps."

He directs us to needy people every day. It might not be as obvious as the story of the Good Samaritan, but the gift of life we receive every day is for his purpose. The more mature you are in the spirit, the clearer you will see God speaking to you and directing your steps. It is just a matter of time and how faithfully you practice that.

I will share one of the whispers of the spirit that came to me during my difficult time. Knowing God is love, I wake up every day and speak to God and ask for guidance to direct my steps to the person he will put in my path today who needs to feel his love. Keep in mind that when I share God's love with others, I am sharing God. So I start every day looking for someone my spirit tells me who needs God. If I get too busy and overlook someone that my spirit directed me to, God will sometimes thump me on the head (a feeling of guilt) when I miss an opportunity to serve others, which he has planned for me. I know some of us have thicker skulls, so we might need two thumps, but don't strike out; surrender your heart to God, and you will be blessed if it takes three thumps (you are really feeling guilty); it is indicative that your spirit is not connected to the goodness of God, and it is high time you need to work harder on yourself.

The spirit did not just stop there. To help prepare me for my daily service to God, here is a very clear practice the spirit gave me that I'd like to share.

Imagine you wake up tomorrow, and there is a basket lying next to your bed right where you put your feet on the floor. You can't get out of bed without picking the basket up. It is a "love" basket! God fills it every night while you are sleeping. When you start your day, that basket is right there, fully loaded; it is your daily mission to empty it. God has a personal message attached to the basket that reads, "Please empty your basket daily; do not bring it back full." 1 John 4:8: "Whoever does not love, does not know God, because God is love."

As a self-proclaimed "Top Gun for God," I will tell you that you really need to guard your heart and your actions. Satan wishes to keep you from responding to God's spiritual calling and keeps deviating you from his path.

The mention of God's name is very powerful; it is a Satan killer. He runs when you draw close to God. 1 Peter 5: 6-11: "Humble yourselves, therefore, under God's mighty hand, that he may lift you up in due time. Cast all your anxiety on him because he cares for you. Be alert and of sober mind. Your enemy the devil prowls around like a roaring lion looking for someone to devour. Resist him, standing firm in the faith, because you know that the family of believers throughout the world is undergoing the same kind of sufferings. And the God of all grace, who called you to his eternal glory in Christ, after you have suffered a little while, will himself restore you and make you strong, firm and steadfast. To him be the power forever and ever. Amen."

In the case of Top Guns, they go through extensive training where they study the enemy, including the whole man, and specialize in knowing their tactics and weapons systems. They take daily tests to refresh their memory on all the critical areas in order to fly safely and win. They must score 100% to fly and fight. When the time comes for battle, they know their enemy and are ready to jump into the cockpit of their superior fighter jets and defeat the enemy.

What and how much do you know about God and his greatest enemy? What is your armor for defeating your enemy, Satan, the father of lies? Let me answer that for you. Your armor is "Truth!" God makes it clear in Psalm 91:4: "He will cover you with his feathers, and under his wings you will find refuge; his faithfulness will be your shield and rampart."

Remember: You cannot grow in the fruits of the spirit if you do not seek truth.

Chapter 2 - Honest Seekers

For starters, one must be an Honest Seeker of truth to understand the fruits offered by the spirit. In that sense, sincerely seeking God's word is of the utmost importance for achieving success in life.

The phrase "honest seekers of God's word" refers to individuals who approach the study of the Bible, or God's teachings, with sincerity, humility, and a genuine desire to understand God's divine truths. I characterize these people by their openness to learning truth, willingness to be transformed by the truths of God's wisdom they discover, and then a commitment to following God's roadmap for life. They prioritize truth over personal biases or preconceived notions. They seek not to justify their own views but to align themselves with God's wisdom and guidance.

I describe an "honest seeker" as someone who prayerfully studies the Bible, thoughtfully considers different perspectives, and discerns truth through the guidance of the Holy Spirit. God describes them in the Bible in scriptures as like:

Jeremiah 29:13: "You will seek me and find me when you seek me with all your heart."

Matthew 5:6: "Blessed are those who hunger and thirst for righteousness, for they will be filled."

It is my understanding that this mindset is also about a pursuit that keeps on going and is not a one-time event, as believers continue to grow in wisdom and fruits of the spirit throughout their spiritual journey.

The truth is not grey. It comes from God and is very clear. God is pure; there are not any shades of grey in his truths. John 14:6 "Jesus told him, "I am the way, the truth, and the life. No one comes to the Father except through me."

Our daily purpose is to be a mirror of God's love in the world of darkness. You cannot defeat the enemy if you are not walking in the truth, and that's a fact.

Could you score 100% on a truth test of God's word? If you are walking on truth, you will reflect the great qualities of the fruits of the spirit. The mature fruits of the spirit are the perfection of God living within us. If we are filled with truth, we will only then be effective in reflecting the light of God into the world of darkness. Adopting the fruits of the spirit into our lives is extremely important when we are trying to teach others about God and his love.

Sometimes, just a small dose of God's love can have a great impact on someone's life, especially someone who has sunken deep in the mire of the world of darkness. It is like dropping a drop of white paint into a cup of black paint. That little drop changes the paint forever in transforming ways that cannot be undone. That's what God's love does; his love changes people's life forever. Love puts God in your heart to be reflected into the world and that is powerful.

Ephesians 6:10-20 (NIV) describes how important it is for us to daily put on the whole armor of God like a Top Gun, getting ready for combat: "Finally, be strong in the Lord and in his mighty power. Put on the full armor of God, so that you can take your stand against the devil's schemes. For our struggle is not against flesh and blood, but against the rulers, against the authorities, against the powers of this dark world and against the spiritual forces of evil in the heavenly realms. Therefore put on the full armor of God, so that when the day of evil comes, you may be able to stand your ground, and after you have done everything, to stand. Stand firm then, with the belt of truth buckled around your waist, with the breastplate of righteousness in place, and with your feet fitted with the readiness that comes from the gospel of peace. In addition to all this, take up the shield of faith, with which you can extinguish all the flaming arrows of the evil one. Take the helmet of salvation and the sword of the Spirit, which is the word of God.

And pray in the Spirit on all occasions with all kinds of prayers and requests. With this in mind, be alert and always keep on praying for all the Lord's people. Pray also for me, that whenever I speak, words may be given me so that I will fearlessly make known the mystery of the gospel, for which I am an ambassador in chains. Pray that I may declare it fearlessly, as I should."

A number of people may know God and be familiar fruits of the spirit, but these fruits have no roots in their souls. Their behaviors are very inconsistent with God's word. They could be referred to as "Dishonest Seekers," people who know God but they do not seek to succumb to his teachings. And because of that, no one desires to be like them, and so they will not see any fruit growing on their tree. Matthew 7:16 (NIV): "By their fruit you will recognize them."

But the Honest Seekers of truth will be in sync with God and will produce much fruit and will be blessed by God in the end.

How does God describe the actions of the dishonest seeker? Just look at James 1:5-8: "If any of you lacks wisdom, you should ask God, who gives generously to all without finding fault, and it will be given to you. But when you ask, you must believe and not doubt, because the one who doubts is like a wave of the sea, blown and tossed by the wind. That person should not expect to receive anything from the Lord. Such a person is double-minded and unstable in all they do."

It is impossible to please God if you can't make up your mind about him being real or not. A double-minded soul struggles with the certainty of his presence, and their actions often reflect it. So, what does a double-minded soul look like? These are the people who love themselves more than others. Their soul misses peace, and joy is rarely seen in their lives. They are impatient and seldom kind to others; goodness is more like an act for them—usually seen when they want something from you. You will often find them justifying why the fellowship of other Christians is not necessary. They lack the tendency to handle situations with a gentle spirit and display very little self-control, yet they claim to be a Christian and a faithful follower of Christ.

I recently ran across a letter on the internet that was supposed to have been written by Lieserl Einstein, the daughter of Albert Einstein, one of the great minds of modern times. This was a personal but powerful letter he supposedly wrote that reflected his acknowledgment of God as love. I refer to this letter with caution as I could not confirm the source of the letter. However, the universal truths in the letter clearly reflected the powerful understanding of the boundless power of the love of God. So, I present the letter for its recognition of God being love, more than it being a factual letter written by Albert Einstein to his daughter.

"When I proposed the theory of relativity, very few understood me, and what I will reveal now to transmit to mankind will also collide with the misunderstanding and prejudice in the world.

I ask you to guard the letters as long as necessary, years, decades until society is advanced enough to accept what I will explain below.

There is an extremely powerful force that, so far, science has not found a formal explanation. It is a force that includes and governs all others, and is even behind any phenomenon operating in the universe and has not yet been identified by us. This universal force is LOVE (God confirms this to be true in his Book of Truth)

When scientists looked for a unified theory of the universe, they forgot the most powerful unseen force.

Love is light that enlightens those who give and receive it.

Love is gravity because it makes some people feel attracted to others.

Love is power because it multiplies the best we have and allows humanity not to be extinguished in their blind selfishness. Love unfolds and reveals.

For love, we live and die.

Love is God, and God is love.

This force explains everything and gives meaning to life. This is the variable that we have ignored for too long, maybe because we are afraid of love because it is the only energy in the universe that man has not learned to drive at will.

To give visibility to love, I made a simple substitution in my most famous equation. If instead of $E = mc^2$, we accept that the energy to heal the world can be obtained through love multiplied by the speed of light squared, we conclude that love is the most powerful force there is because it has no limits.

After the failure of humanity in the use and control of the other forces of the universe that have turned against us, we must nourish ourselves with another kind of energy...

If we want our species to survive, if we are to find meaning in life, if we want to save the world and every sentient being that inhabits it, love is the only answer.

Perhaps we are not yet ready to make a bomb of love, a device powerful enough to destroy the hate, selfishness, and greed that devastate the planet.

However, each individual carries within them a small but powerful generator of love whose energy is waiting to be released.

When we learn to give and receive this universal energy, dear Lieserl, we will have affirmed that love conquers all and is able to transcend everything and anything because love is the quintessence of life.

I deeply regret not having been able to express what is in my heart, which has quietly beated for you all my life. Maybe it's too late to apologize, but as time is relative, I need to tell you that I love you, and thanks to you, I have reached the ultimate answer!"

~Your father, Albert Einstein.

Regardless of who wrote the letter, the truths it revealed were very real: God is love, and love is God, and love is the most powerful force in the universe. Life without Love is a black hole filled with darkness, a place where God never goes. Without God, there is no life. So, our greatest human need as creations of God is to connect with God and his glorious love. God said in Genesis 2:18 that a single spirit was not good: "The Lord God said, 'It is not good for the man to be alone. I will make a helper suitable for him.'"

We cannot share the love of God living alone. God mentions "wives" over 325 times in his word to reinforce the fact that he intended for a man and a woman to be joined in marriage. They become one with each other, and God repeats the importance of this commitment in both the Old and New Testaments.

Genesis 2:24: "That is why a man leaves his father and mother and is united to his wife, and they become one flesh."

Matthew 19:5: "and said, 'For this reason a man will leave his father and mother and be united to his wife, and the two will become one flesh?"

Ephesians 5:31: "For this reason a man shall leave his father and mother and be joined to his wife, and the two shall become one flesh."

The triad of love between husband, wife, and God is one of the most powerful forces in the universe to project God's light into the world of darkness effectively. That is why it is important when a person is seeking a soulmate for life that their mate must be equally and deeply rooted in the fruits of the spirit. I do not suggest them to be perfect, but I do recommend that they should be staunch in the pursuit of fulfilling their God-given role of being a mirror of God's love in the world, spreading kindness, and exhibiting gentle nature.

In the next chapter, I will share my journey toward knowing God, the history of my life with my first soulmate, and the sad ending of losing her. It was during those dark days that I discovered God's Hands of Love, and that became my source of inspiration.

Chapter 3 - My God Connection

My church memories date back to when I was only four years old. My family occasionally attended a small country Baptist church (St. John Baptist Church). We were not consistent in attendance, as my dad was an alcoholic, and it depended on whether he had been sober long enough that he felt okay to attend the mass.

When we attended, my mom and a lady named Mrs. Moore taught Sunday school classes for us kids. I still remember the little one-page Bible story handouts, our hand fans, the cookies, and the Kool-Aid we got each week for behaving well. During those Bible classes at a very early age (around 4-6), I started knowing Jesus and the sacrifices he made for the world. I instantly felt a connection with Jesus and sang the song "Jesus Loves Me" enough times to believe it in my heart. And yes, I drank the Kool-Aid and ate the cookies, too; that was our reward for being good during the lessons!

I grew up knowing and loving God but drifted away during my early days serving in the United States Air Force. However, my renewed commitment to Christ began at the Williams Road Church of Christ in Columbus, Ohio, in September 1970. I was a sergeant in the Air Force, 21 years old, stationed at Lockbourne Air Force Base in Columbus, Ohio, and I began having a strong calling to return to my faith in God from my boyhood days.

The first time I attended Williams Road COC, the pastor, Ray Humphries, led the Wednesday Bible study in the auditorium. He was teaching from the book of Romans, Chapter 8. The message was about how good life would be if the spirit led it and how bad it could be if led by the carnal mind. I felt as if that message was presented just for me. I knew God and could distinguish right from wrong, but I had not committed to walking in the light.

My heart picked that message, and that night, and I decided I wanted the spirit to lead me. I started attending church on Sunday mornings and Wednesday evenings regularly, and soon thereafter, a God story was created, and something really special happened.

On a Wednesday night before Thanksgiving in November 1970, I met my spiritual soulmate and wife-to-be, Luana Jean Coon (Jeannie). When I looked back on my start at Williams Road, I realized it was no coincidence that God led me to that small little congregation.

She was home on Thanksgiving break from her senior year at Harding University in Searcy, Arkansas. She had a special glow, and I was immediately attracted to her. I felt like the angels were singing, and the bells were ringing all around her as she lit up the auditorium with her presence.

I did not know that night would be the biggest life-changing moment of my life, and from that meeting we would fall in love and live happily in serving God together for 49 years, but God did.

Neither did I know that I would take her home that night after the youth gathering at the Thompson house (Jeannie in Yellow Jumper and me at the bottom with the youngster).

The same night, I got an introduction to the game of "spoons." And I saw that beautiful, young, spirited woman enjoying that game. I was so glad she sat at the opposite end of the table from me so I could look at her all night. I enjoyed having big folding bench seats in my Chevrolet Malibu, and that she sat in the middle next to me in my car while I drove her home that night.

Also, the next day, she took my call and accepted my offer for our first official date on Friday night.

To my delight, she was very flexible with me as the car show I planned on taking her to turned out not to be at the fairgrounds for another two weeks.

I loved that she could be happy with simple things, like having a pizza and talking for hours. I still remember how glad I was to be with her. God spoke to me that night, revealing that this precious soul would need someone to protect her, love her, and help lead her to heaven. I did not tell her, but I accepted that role even before we finished our pizza that night. However, my strategy to get there was far from being in place.

During her Thanksgiving break, I had two dates with this beautiful lady, Jeannie. On Sunday, she left to return to Harding University for end-of-semester exams. She was a senior, so I just hoped God was not teasing me, because I felt she was the one for me!

She returned home the week before Christmas and attended my 4th Jule Miller Bible study lesson on Sunday evening at the Thompson's home, December 20, 1970. I was so glad she was there as I decided to be baptized that night.

After my baptism, I felt a burning desire to share the "good news" with my parents in Frankfort, Kentucky. So, on Saturday, December 26th, Jeannie and I made a round trip from Columbus to Frankfort and back to share this joyous news with them. After lunch, a fried rabbit cooked by my dad—and a brief visit with my parents, I gave Jeannie a quick tour of the Capitol building and one of Frankfort's notable landmarks, Daniel Boone's grave.

That may sound like a "deadbeat" date, but Daniel Boone was more than just a historical figure to us country boys. He was an important American frontiersman and explorer, a true model of being a "real man."

After her excitement came down from visiting Daniel Boone's memorial tombstone overlooking the beautiful, winding Kentucky River, we left Frankfort and drove to Georgetown, where we stopped for coffee. I drove to the first rest area on I-75 to drink coffee and spend more time with Jeannie before I hit the interstate. I enjoyed more time with Jeannie and connecting with her beautiful spirit.

It was a perfect day for our visit, with really great weather for a winter day in December. As we sat and talked, I told Jeannie it sure was a BEAUTIFUL day, and she said yes it was. I said, "Don't you wish all your days could be as BEAUTIFUL as this?" Much to my surprise, she responded, "Is that a proposal?" Being a really smart Kentucky boy, I knew that was my moment. I quickly said yes, and she said yes!!! We kissed, and I thought I just got engaged on MY THIRD date!!! It was great. I wanted it in my heart, but I might have planned it a little differently if I was actually planning the engagement. I didn't know I would get engaged this way, but God did. And I bet he laughed!!!

In the future, whenever we use the word 'beautiful', it would always make us smile and laugh together. Before Jeannie passed, I wrote a poem for her describing the beauty I saw in her from the word BEAUTIFUL.

Jeannie Reed

My beautiful wife and friend for life. Don't you wish all your days could be as "beautiful" as this? Here is the "beautiful" I see in you.

B – Best gift God ever gave to me.

E – Every day is better than the day before.

A – Amazing love for God, family, and everyone.

U – Unmatched energy for service to others.

T – Tender love for children.

I – Incredible sports fan.

F – Friendliest person I know.

U – Unflappable in her faith.

L – Loves with all her heart.

Because you are so BEAUTIFUL I will love you for eternity.

Just a short time before Jeannie's passing, a special family friend wrote these BEAUTIFUL words for us.

ONE BEAUTIFUL DAY

A love between a teacher and a "Shadow."

Set an example for us all to follow.

A love so deep, steadfast, and pure,

A love that cares, praises and cures.

Together a team that walks hand in hand,

A Love created by the mighty maker of man.

A love that brought, Jenny, Kim and Jon and many generations to come,

A love filled with faith and trust, in "They will be done".

Thank you for sharing this family you have made,

All because of one most BEAUTIFUL DAY.

After we were engaged, I got to say "I love you" for the first time!!! Although this was not the ideal model I would suggest to anyone but with God's blessings it lasted 49 happy, beautiful years of my life. Our spirits were both focused on pleasing God with our lives, which was exactly why God brought us together. I realized later that this was one of the best God stories of my life.

Now that I was a Christian and engaged to my future wife, I had a good reason to consider changing my life plans. I applied for the Air Force early out program to go to school and was accepted. So, in January 1971, I left the Air Force and enrolled in Harding University as a freshman while Jeannie finished her senior year. I majored in the Bible because I felt a strong calling to preach God's word from my baptism. This was Jeannie and me in one of the Harding Love swings. This photo was in the front of the 1971 Harding yearbook.

I loved my time at Harding, especially my great Bible teachers, meeting all of Jeannie's friends, sitting in Chapel and singing with what seemed to be earth angels. The food was also good at the Harding Heritage Cafeteria, I think they had the best coconut cream pie ever, I ate it every day for lunch. Harding left such a strong impression on my spirit that we sent all three kids there to get a good Christian education.

On June 5th, 1971, Jeannie and I married at the Williams Road Church of Christ, which was truly a great moment in my life.

I was still a young man, 22 years old, but felt really called to serve God. I started out leading youth programs, teaching Bible classes, and occasionally preaching for small overseas military congregations and churches in Texas and Florida, and leading home Bible studies for 20 years. I was ordained as an Elder in the Church of Christ and in a Christian Church.

After 49 great years of life together, on July 29, 2020, Jeannie passed away in our home of 30 years and set off to enjoy her eternal rewards.

We raised three adult kids, and today, they all live within one to two hours apart in Central Florida. Our home in Eustis served God's family for 34 years hosting many fellowships, Bible classes, baptisms, and an overflowing of God's love.

In 2024, for the first time in 54 years, our family no longer met at the home in Eustis for the Thanksgiving holidays. My daughter Kim started the transition in hosting our family gatherings, and I was her guest. It was a beautiful transition.

Together, Jeannie and I shared five grandchildren: two grandsons, Zane, 17, and Reese, 15, from my daughter Kim, and three granddaughters, Kaley, 26, Ansley, 24, and Kinsley, 21, from my daughter Jenny, still waiting on my son, Jon, to add to the family.

I am honored to claim the joy of 3 John 1:4: "I have no greater joy than to hear that my children walk in truth." All of my kids and grands are baptized believers. I had the pleasure of baptizing my two daughters in South Carolina and my grandson Zane in the lake behind our house. That was a great day on Lake Louise!

Here is the poem I would dedicate to that home.

This Old House

This old house was just a place that we found to live one day,

It was built of concrete blocks, nothing special in any way.

It sat upon a small lake with a small dock at the time,

It even had a swimming pool, for the days the sun did shine.

A house does not give you any love or respect,

It cannot mend a soul or help a wrecked life.

But when occupied with God's family, the house seems to come to life,

It appears to have a glow and a heart that makes things feel right.

The reputation of this house seemed to build with each passing year,

It was known for hospitality and bringing families lots of joy and cheer.

With friendly hospitality and love for all that came through its doors,

It became a special place to feel loved, and no one kept any scores.

The Mom and the Dad were always sharing God's precious love,

It soon was apparent to all that it was coming down from above.

The mom, who was the hostess, served God's love to all that came,

All her guests loved her, which is how this old house got its fame.

The mom was a teacher and was known throughout the town,

She had loved many children and lifted many frowns.

She was a great encourager, one who would always go the extra mile,

Just to make someone's day better and try to make them smile.

This special home would change with the seasons as its hostess loved them all,

She had lots of decorations, some big and some quite small.

They all seemed to say this is a happy place to be,

Because God gives us seasons to enjoy new scenery.

She kept an accurate calendar of all her friend's special days,

That included birthdays and anniversaries that seemed to pass by like a blaze.

Her warm and tender heart made her guest excited to come in,

Whether Sports, birthday parties, or Bible studies, no one wanted them to end.

This old house taught many people God's precious Word throughout the years,

It baptized young and old and helped dry up many tears.

Someday, this family will leave this old house, and the stories will be told,

How they loved so many people, and for Jesus, they stood bold.

Many children and puppies have run and played in its backyard,

For all those special memories will make leaving it very hard.

This old house is just a building that can be used for many things,

We hope it continues to serve God's children and helps them get their wings.

God, thank you for the blessings you give us every day,

Thank you for this old house we got to use along our way.

Happy Mother's Day 2020 to the one who made "This Old House" so special.

Luana Jean "Jeannie" Reed.

Love You Forever,

Husband and Dad of This Old House

Chapter 4 - My Days of Sadness

From Right to Left: Senior High School, College Senior, Marriage, Teacher days, Retirement, last Christmas 2019 and last golf Tournament January 2020

On July 29, 2020, that was the day my wife left this world. After 49 years, one month, and 24 days of life with a wonderful Christian wife, God finally took her back home. I was stranded, all alone, on the journey of life. During this time, the "Hands of Love" concept emerged—a spirit-led inspiration that God slowly imparted to me when I began my search for a new soulmate.

No matter what you do, there is no way to prepare yourself for that season of life. I was lost and confused, uncertain of where my life would go and what I would do. I spent a lot of time just writing and expressing my feelings. I had written a song for Jeannie before she passed. I would look at these seven photos covering different phases of her life and play that song daily for days, weeks, and months. I would share the song and her pictures with anyone visiting me. I did not know why I felt compelled to do that; I just felt good sharing Jeannie with others.

I share the lyrics to the song in this book because I think someone reading this story has felt similar pains, and hopefully, the words will inspire the soul that may have lost their soulmate, and these words might reflect feelings in your heart.

My Precious Wife
By David Reed – 5-12-2019

My life before I met her felt empty in every way.

I had no vision for my life, I had not found my way.

Although my life was active and I was a strong and healthy man,

There seemed to be a barrier that was blocking my life's plan.

Then the day God sent her, my life changed in every way.

My empty feelings left me, and joy now filled my day.

A happy man she made me the day she came into life,

God sent His blessings to me when He made her my wife.

The loving smile upon her face and the sparkle in her eye,

Warmed my heart, and changed my life, and now I am flying high.

Her love is pure as an angel, she made my life feel whole,

I finally had a clear vision in the way my life would go.

Thank you, Jeannie, for loving me, and being my precious wife.

Her love for God, and for me, and our precious family,

Showed others how to live this life to be sure of their eternity.

Her love has touched many people and they will never forget,

How her pure, and loving heart, kept them from many regrets.

Her walk with God and trust in him has been a great example for all,

I know our Father is pleased with her and how she answered his call.

Although her life is over and from us, she did depart,

The memories of her precious love will be in our hearts.

The loving smile upon her face and the sparkle in her eye,

Warmed my heart, and changed my life, and now I am flying high.

Her love is pure as an angel, she made my life feel whole,

I finally had a clear vision in the way my life would go.

Thank you, Jeannie, for loving me, and being my precious wife.

Through all our years together, she was a perfect mom and wife,

She taught her students to love God, and to try and live a good life.

She had lots of fun playing golf and dining with family and friends,

And she can play her card games until the nighttime ends.

When the seasons for her football and other sports come around,

She loves to decorate our house and some things even make sounds.

As a hostess for many people that come into our home,

She makes them all feel special as if they sat upon a throne.

The loving smile upon her face and the sparkle in her eye,

Warmed my heart, and changed my life, and now I am flying high.

Her love is pure as an angel, she made my life feel whole,

I finally had a clear vision in the way my life would go.

Thank you, Jeannie, for loving me, and being my precious wife.

Thank you, Jeannie, for 50 BEAUTIFUL years,

and a very WONDERFUL LIFE.

Thank you, sweetie, I love you very much, and I will see you soon.

As I would sing this song and dive into my deep sadness, I would hear her voice say, "Life is for the Living; move on, and Go, Bucs!!!" She loved her football!

After several months of being sad and confused, I asked myself that very difficult question: How long do I stay in this tragic state of life? Is there a time limit? If so, how do you transition back to a normal life? What is normal now?

Although we had aged, our spirits still felt very young at heart. How do you replace a beautiful wife, friend, sports fan, soulmate, and all the memories you shared over almost 50 years? These were all questions that needed clarity for my soul.

God's answer was very simple. "You grieve until you are ready to move on. The key word was YOU! I realized there was no time limit, but I was free to make the transition whenever I felt living in the past was no longer where I wanted to be.

You cannot live in the past; you can linger in it and keep yourself miserable as often, or as long as YOU decide. You can't change the past! You live life daily and choose to enjoy the blessing of life every day that God gives you. I realized there were no set timelines for anyone to linger in the grieving season, so I continued talking with God daily until He gave me the clarity I needed to move on.

But before that clarity came, I had bottomed out with my emotions several times and had written a poem that describes my feelings, entitled "Bottom of the Sea." If you have lost a loved one, you too may have had similar feelings.

Bottom of the Sea

*When I would wake up in the morning and see the lovely smile upon
her face*

I would thank my God for putting me in this very special place.

Holding her close every morning and every night before we slept,

*And kissing her sweet lips would remind me of the beautiful promises
that we kept.*

Our spirits were so beautiful and such a perfect blend,

We were truly a match made in heaven, and we never wanted it to end.

When I look back on the day that God took her from me,

*It felt like someone tied me to an anchor and dropped me to the bottom
of the sea.*

Oh, I tried so hard to surface as each day went passing by,

But the pressure was too great so I would just sit there and cry.

I would think of all the good times and play her special song,

I would start early each morning and some days play it all day long.

*Days and weeks and months passed by, And I did not know what I
should do,*

*I would hear her voice saying, "Life is for the Living," so it is all up to
you.*

*When you feel like your life has left you, and you are all alone at the
bottom of the sea,*

You ask, why did God just take her, why didn't He also take me.

The direction of my life seemed so uncertain, so vague, and so unclear,

But I know my good Shepherd tells me that He is always very near.

So, I had to put my trust in the one who made the sky and sea,

For He will remove all my hurt and He will come and rescue me.

As I look to my future and the path He has prepared for me,

I humbly try to serve Him, and in turn, He lifts me from the bottom of the sea.

I am sure many who have lost a beautiful soulmate have been there and can relate.

Shortly after I started my ascent back to a normal life, I faced the challenge of going through our 50th wedding anniversary alone. Jeannie and I had planned to renew our wedding vows on our 50th. She still had her wedding dress and looked forward to wearing it again.

On June 5th, I pulled the dress out, took some photos, and passed it on to one of my granddaughters. But since it was still a very important date, I wrote another poem honoring my love, which was no longer with me. It was titled: "Golden Anniversary Day."

Golden Anniversary Day

The Fifth day of June was our Wedding Anniversary Day,

The day I married the most beautiful earth angel, as many would likely say.

She had a glow about her, that everyone could vividly see,

I felt so blessed, and honored, that she chose to marry me.

She was so radiant and beautiful, and so loved by all,

I knew her love was real, and that it would never, ever, fall.

We were young and not real sure where our lives would go,

But our faith was strong, so we did not fear, or have a care to know.

We trusted God faithfully from the day that we first met,

Until the day I faced her departure, my life's deepest regret.

We had planned for years what we would do on this special, Golden Day,

We would dress up and renew our vows, as fifty years in marriage is quite rare, if I might say.

Her beautiful wedding dress still hangs in a closet in our old house,

But sad to say, the dress will not be donned, but I had to bring it out.

Her departure does not mean that the Golden joy is not still there,

For having the beautiful life I had with Jeannie, is so very, very, rare.

Knowing she made it to heaven is Golden enough for me,

She now walks the streets of gold, which are far better to see.

I would love to have seen her in that dress and glowing in her special way,

But for now, I am thankful to God for 49 years, one month and 24 beautiful days.

We planned this day to be posting photos of us renewing our vows,

But Proverbs 16:9 makes clear that we make plans, but God directs our steps, to all of life's woes and wows.

Although this day might not go as we had hoped, it is still very special for me,

For I have had the pleasure of many beautiful days, with the beautiful Jeannie Reed.

Happy Golden Anniversary, upon the streets of gold, to my precious Jeannie.

Loving You Forever,

Your Honey Bunny

So, after losing my outstanding wife, and lovely soulmate of 49 years, in July 2020, I was lost and seeking God's help to maneuver through this new season of troubled waters. My big question for God was, how do I seek a new soulmate?

I had not dated in 50 years. I was really lost and felt like my life was sinking. My faith was still strong, but I missed having a soulmate to share life with. I loved when Jeannie would come into my office and sit on my lap so I could give her hugs throughout the day. I loved praying together every morning and every night, hearing her sing when we attended church, and sharing God's love with our family, our church family, and many needy souls.

As I came out of my doldrums, I trusted what Jesus said in Matthew 7:7-8: "Ask, and it will be given to you; seek, and you will find; knock, and it will be opened to you. For everyone who asks receives, and he who seeks finds, and to him who knocks it will be opened."

God's divine spirit responded and gently guided me to my answers. He gave me a vision of the power hidden in the invisible qualities of the hand. God revealed invisible attributes to me, including creating a perfect, eternal oneness with a new soulmate. Hopefully, God's universal message revealed to me will inspire everyone in their marriage and courting relationships to establish strong ETERNAL BONDS according to God's plan.

As I stated earlier, God's inspired message extends beyond just marital bonds. It was also a universal concept that could restore friendships, communities, and even the world God created.

When God began speaking to my spirit, he reminded me that he had the whole world in his hands. His hands kept ringing in my head until I finally raised my hands and stared at them, seeking meaning. I became so curious about the message that I searched Bible Gateway to see how many times God used "hands" in the Bible to make his point. I was amazed when I discovered how many times HANDS were used. Yes, the Biblical count 1416 is the number of times God used hands to make His point.

So, I thought, why wouldn't God use his hands again? I called this inspired message the "Hands of Love" because God led me to this vision through love. He gave me an inspired message to help create and restore relationships to a greater walk with him, my creator, that, if applied according to his design, assures a solid bond with a future soulmate. My story will just provide one more HAND story, making the new count 1,416 plus ONE = 1,417, as seen on my cover.

In Genesis 3:22, the Lord God said, "The man has now become like one of us, knowing good and evil. He must not be allowed to reach out his hand and take also from the tree of life and eat and live forever."

The physical part of man is the hand that cursed man's life upon the earth as he pursued a physical object of the world. But it is the invisible qualities of the hand that God revealed to Jesus and the apostles and a new vision he gave to me to guide my spirit through this difficult season.

We are not predestined robots. God created us for his purpose, yet from the days of Adam and Eve, He gave us the freedom of choice. The word of God assures us that we are universally assisted by God when we call upon his name. I was calling upon His name when my first wife passed, and I wanted direction for my life in my pursuit of a new wife.

As we read in the book of Psalms, Psalms 23:4, God says, "...even though I walk through the valley of the shadow of death, I will fear no evil, for thou art with me...". Knowing God was on my side and that I needed a soulmate to complete me, God sent me a clear message on how to start my search for a new soulmate.

Chapter 5 - My New Inspiration

My Wednesday night Bible Study Group

As the days went by, it became clear that God was speaking to my spirit and telling me to continue teaching my Wednesday night home Bible study that I had been doing for seven years and keep trusting in him. We established our group as the One Love Family Bible Church. Looking back, I remember having around 22 people from five churches attending those classes.

In the photo at the beginning of this chapter, we had just completed Jack Graham's study on the Book of Revelations, and we had Jack on a Zoom call talking with each class member. He was projected on our big screen while our members stood around him.

If I could be faithful and trust God, I knew he would lead me down the path of life he wanted me to go. I was unsure what that would be, but I hoped to find a new soulmate to refresh my soul and complete me. I was looking for someone with whom I could enjoy the rest of my earthly life until I was called to heaven to meet Jesus.

There could never be a replacement for my wife, so my spirit asked God for a new soulmate to refresh my soul with new things I had never experienced. Every day, I devoted my life to trying to please God. I prayed every morning and sought his wisdom and guidance. I wanted to keep my life focused on God and ensure everything I thought, said, and every action I did pleased him.

I knew God expected me to continue to reflect his love and spread light in the world of darkness. To maintain my focus, I imagined that God placed a basket full of love by my bedside every morning and allotted me a mission to empty my basket by spreading his love to as many as I could every day. It was clear that I was to bring my basket back empty every night. While this kept me focused on my service to God, it did not help me understand how to date or seek a soulmate in this season of life.

I was alone for the first time in 50 years. I did not know how to date as I had no experience reaching out and connecting with a woman. Remember, my last engagement was effortless and came after three dates!

I prayed daily for God's wisdom in seeking the right spiritual soulmate. My three adult kids were all advising me on how to connect online. Both of my daughters had gone through a divorce, and my son was still single, so it felt weird that we were all single at the same time. We joked about starting a pool, and the first one married won the prize. And guess who won!

It took about one year of asking every day before God filled my spirit with the guidance I needed to complete my search for a new soulmate.

After a while of searching, God revealed to my spirit a remarkable inspiration of his great wisdom that I called "The Hands of Love." God knew my needs and what he had planned for my future. I just had to pray, seek, trust, and wait upon God to deliver. It is so comforting to know that in times like these; my life could rest in the powerful and loving hands of a personable God who truly cares for me and has a plan for my life. His previous plan for my life was BEAUTIFUL, so I had great hopes for my future.

In John 16:12-14, God makes clear that he speaks to us through the Holy Spirit. "I have much more to say to you, more than you can now bear. But when he, the Spirit of truth, comes, he will guide you into all the truth. He will not speak on his own; he will speak only what he hears, and he will tell you what is yet to come. He will glorify me because it is from me that he will receive what he will make known to you."

God has clarified that all truth comes from him to us through the Holy Spirit. Many things look like truth, but a tint of darkness at the core makes those things impure and unacceptable to God. I want all my readers to know that I have asked God to guide me in everything I say in this book to ensure I only present what God calls truth.

I hope this book will inspire all readers to see how the Hands of God/Love take on many roles; however, every action involves love. He is your creator, strength, protector, and guide to an everlasting life. We also hope this book will paint a clear pathway for everyone seeking to create an eternal bond with their existing or future soulmate and God. Eternal commitments to God and your soulmate will last forever, meaning nothing can sever these unbreakable bonds.

Ultimately, God wants our spirits to survive this world's temptations and darkness and stay with him eternally. But we all know that from the beginning of time, Satan has sought to destroy our relationship with God by luring us into the dark world of sin to please the desires of the flesh and to block our spiritual connection with God. Genesis 3:22 and the Lord God said: "The man has now become like one of us, knowing good and evil. He must not be allowed to reach out his hand and take also from the tree of life and eat and live forever."

When Adam and Eve allowed their hands to participate in Satan's evil scheme, they chose the pleasures of sin over being obedient to God. They decided the Hands of Evil over the Hands of Love. Their physical hands played a very important role in man's fall. We hope the wisdom that God has imparted to me, presented in this book, will help you avoid Satan's snares so that you and your soulmate may have spirits aligned as one, be victorious, and live eternally with God.

In Proverbs 16:9, God directs our steps: "In his heart a man will plan his course, but the Lord will direct his steps." The Book of Truth, God's Holy Word, clarifies how God had a plan for us before his hands placed us in our mother's womb. It means that when we choose to follow God, every step we take in our lives is a part of the God story he had planned for us. Jeremiah 1:5: "Before I formed you in the womb I knew you, before you were born, I set you apart; I appointed you as a prophet to the nations." So, before God placed me into my mother's womb, he had a plan for me, and I know for certain that the "Hands of Love" was a part of his plan for my life. Jeannie's departure was intended to open a new door for me, allowing me an opportunity to love another person in this life and help by leading them to heaven.

Let me illustrate the Hands of Love for you. God put my hands together when this inspiration came, and the spirit started speaking to me. He made clear that there are three distinct phases in building a lasting relationship:

The Attraction Phase deals with physical appearance (the five attractions that you look for in a person to date)

The Connection Phase involves a deep examination of your future soulmate's spirit to see if the fruits of the spirit are present. They are the invisible qualities of the soul (the spaces between your fingers where the Hands of Love concept describes the building block approach for the invisible qualities of the spirit)

The Bonding Phase describes where the two hands connect and become one. It is an advancement of the deep search of the spirit to where the palms are touching (and the fingers can now interlock onto the hand of your soulmate), and God seals the bond and the relationship.

There are nine invisible qualities or fruits of the spirit. Galatians 5:22-23: "But the fruit of the spirit is love, joy, peace, forbearance, kindness, goodness, faithfulness, gentleness, and self-control." We will cover these nine fruits of the spirit in separate chapters. They are arranged in the order in which your life grows as you submit to Christ and begin following the truths of God's word.

Here is a quick synopsis of the "Hands of Love" inspiration. Relationships built on attractions alone are easily broken, but those who search the invisible qualities of the soul for the fruits of the spirit and "find them" have a solid foundation for establishing a deep connection that will provide a platform for creating a bond that God can approve; one that will last forever.

Furthermore, God clarifies that wise soul searching can lead to strong spiritual connections and bonds that cannot be easily broken. That is God's desire for all of us. Matthew 19:6: "What God joined together, let no one separate."

In the next two chapters, I will illustrate the Hands of Love in more detail when I cover attraction, connection, and bonding.

Let us now review the ATTRACTION phase.

Chapter 6 - The Attraction

The attraction phase is important in finding a soulmate but can also destroy you. It is true to say that attraction is an important factor FOR ME, but it is not the only thing that keeps the bond strong in a relationship between a husband and wife.

Two types of spirits are always at work. The spirit of the flesh tells you to go for physical things like beauty, a great body, the fashion dresser, the driver of the luxury car, the one with the big bank account, the superior upscale living conditions, or just a great appetite for sex.

The second spirit is the spirit of God. It speaks directly to our spirit and encourages us to seek the invisible fruits of the spirit in our soulmates, which are everlasting and in sync with God. Romans 6:13-14: "Therefore do not let sin reign in your mortal body so that you obey its evil desires. Do not offer any part of yourself to sin as an instrument of wickedness, but rather offer yourselves to God as those who have been brought from death to life; and offer every part of yourself to him as an instrument of righteousness."

As a man of God, I wanted to respect my Savior, Jesus, and myself as much, if not more, than my potential soulmate. I must live the fruits of the spirit to be a good match for the spiritual woman I am pursuing.

I Thessalonians 4:3-8: "It is God's will that you should be sanctified: that you should avoid sexual immorality; that each of you should learn to control your own body in a way that is holy and honorable, not in passionate lust like the pagans, who do not know God; and that in this matter no one should wrong or take advantage of a brother or sister. The Lord will punish all those who commit such sins, as we told you and warned you before. For God did not call us to be impure, but to live a holy life. Therefore, anyone who rejects this instruction does not reject a human being but God, the very God who gives you his Holy Spirit."

These words clearly show everyone that when we submit to God, he expects us to live a pure life. Your soulmate should reflect an honest pursuit of a mature and pure spirit, as described in I Corinthians 13.

1 Corinthians 13, often referred to as the "Love Chapter," provides a profound description of love and its qualities. Below is an in-depth look at each quality mentioned in this passage:

1. Patient

• Description: Patience is the ability to endure difficult circumstances, delays, or annoyances without becoming frustrated or angry. It involves a willingness to wait and to tolerate imperfections in others.

• In Practice: A patient person gives others the time they need to grow and change. They don't rush to judgment and are willing to listen and understand rather than react impulsively.

2. Kind

• Description: Kindness involves being considerate, compassionate, and generous toward others. It reflects a genuine concern for the well-being of others and a desire to help.

• In Practice: Kindness can be shown through small acts of service, encouraging words, or simply being there for someone in need. It's about treating others with respect and warmth.

3. Not Envious

• Description: Love does not envy or covet what others have. It celebrates the success and happiness of others rather than feeling resentful or jealous.

• In Practice: An unselfish love rejoices in the achievements and good fortune of others, recognizing that their happiness does not diminish one's own worth or value.

4. Not Boastful

• Description: Love does not seek to draw attention to oneself or brag about achievements. It is humble and does not inflate one's own importance.

- In Practice: A loving person acknowledges their strengths and accomplishments without overshadowing others. They recognize that true value comes from within and not from accolades.

5. Not Proud

- Description: Love is not arrogant or haughty. It does not elevate oneself above others or consider oneself superior.

- In Practice: Humility is a key aspect of love. A loving individual respects others and values their contributions, understanding that everyone has unique worth.

6. Not Rude

- Description: Love does not behave in a disrespectful or offensive manner. It is considerate of others' feelings and maintains a sense of decorum.

- In Practice: A loving person communicates with respect and thoughtfulness, avoiding harsh words or actions that could hurt others.

7. Not Self-Seeking

- Description: Love is not selfish or focused solely on one's own interests. It seeks the good of others and prioritizes their needs over personal desires.

- In Practice: A selfless love is willing to make sacrifices for the sake of others, demonstrating a commitment to their happiness and well-being.

8. Not Easily Angered

- Description: Love is slow to anger and does not react with hostility or frustration at the slightest provocation. It maintains a sense of calm and composure.

- In Practice: A loving person takes the time to understand the situation before reacting, practicing forgiveness and understanding rather than holding onto grudges.

9. Keeps No Record of Wrongs

- Description: Love does not hold onto past grievances or keep score of offenses. It forgives and moves on rather than dwelling on past mistakes.

- In Practice: A loving individual chooses to let go of hurt and resentment, fostering an environment of trust and healing in relationships.

10. Rejoices with the Truth

- Description: Love celebrates honesty and truthfulness. It values integrity and aligns itself with what is right and just.

- In Practice: A loving person encourages open and honest communication, supporting others in their pursuit of truth and righteousness.

11. Always Protects

- Description: Love is protective and seeks to safeguard the well-being of others. It stands up for and defends those it cares about.

- In Practice: A loving individual provides emotional support and security, ensuring that their loved ones feel safe and valued.

12. Always Trusts

- Description: Love is built on trust and confidence in others. It believes in the best in people and is willing to take risks in relationships.

- In Practice: A trusting love fosters openness and vulnerability, creating a strong bond between individuals.

13. Always Hopes

- Description: Love maintains hope and optimism, believing in the potential for growth and positive change. It does not give up easily.

- In Practice: A loving person encourages others to strive for their goals and dreams, providing support and motivation even in difficult times.

14. Always Perseveres

- Description: Love endures through challenges and hardships. It is steadfast and committed, refusing to give up on those it cares about.

- In Practice: A persevering love stands strong in the face of adversity, demonstrating loyalty and dedication regardless of circumstances.

Conclusion

The qualities of love described in 1 Corinthians 13 emphasize a selfless, enduring, and compassionate approach to relationships. By embodying these traits, individuals can cultivate deeper connections and foster a loving environment in their lives. Love, as portrayed in this passage, is not merely a feeling but a choice and a commitment to act in ways that uplift and support others.

We all have sinned and come short of the glory of God. Great news: if we seek Christ, we can all be forgiven. The scar remains with you, but God sets your spirit free to allow you to move forward with your life. The Christians desire to keep their memories good, so they follow Psalm 119:10: "I seek you with all my heart; do not let me stray from your commands." The apostle Paul warned the early Christians in 1 Corinthians 10:12: "So, if you think you are standing firm, be careful that you don't fall!" We will all stumble, as none of us are perfect. Matthew 5:28: "You have heard that it was said, 'You shall not commit adultery.' But I tell you that anyone who looks at a woman lustfully has already committed adultery with her in his heart." God does not want any bad thoughts lingering in the Holy Spirit he placed in us.

God makes clear his position in Hebrews 13:4: "Marriage should be honored by all, and the marriage bed kept pure, for God will judge the adulterer and all the sexually immoral." Because the scars of sexual immorality can remain with us for a lifetime, God wants us to stay pure before entering into marriage.

We have all heard it said that beauty lies in the eyes of the beholder! Satan loves to use that beauty to entrap you. But beauty can be elusive. It can change with seasons through sickness, accidents, stress, or just poor nurturing as you go down the pathway of life.

Relationships built solely on attractions could easily end when change comes, and the beauty fades. I watched my beautiful wife become a different person as her cancer, in its later days, changed her lovely, happy face to one that was swollen to an unrecognizable, altering her beautiful spirit in a way that saddened me to my heart. Yet, my love for her grew stronger as all I could see was that beautiful spirit I connected with on a BEAUTIFUL day in December of 1970 that was now on its way to see Jesus.

When widows, widowers, or divorcees begin searching for a soulmate, there are typically five main points of attraction. These may not always be stated explicitly, but they are present in the person you wish to date.

Before I explain the attraction phase and cover my five personal attraction features, let me make a clear point for those who have lost a soulmate.

You need to grieve. At some point, ask yourself, "Am I trying to live in the past?" That is a very important question. When you realize that is what you are doing, ask yourself, "When did I start living in the present?" That is where you can start serving God. You can't serve God if you remain in the past. Your time with the soulmate that God gave you is over. Hopefully, it was a great blessing for you. But now a new door is opening for you, your future. This door is open for you to seek another soulmate to finish your journey here. God said it is not good for man to be alone.

Take note of this VERY IMPORTANT statement that Jesus made in Matthew 22:30: "At the resurrection people will neither marry nor be given in marriage; they will be like the angels in heaven." So your past is your past. Your journey and the blessings of the past are behind you. The blessings and joy for the rest of your life are in front of you, not behind you. It is up to you what way you choose.

We all live day by day until we are called home to be with Jesus. If you have one, two, or even three soulmates in your journey up until here, feel blessed that God is using you to help another soul on their journey to heaven.

Now, imagine that both the male and the female are represented if you look at your fingertips on each hand. You will be represented by the fingertips on your right hand, and your soulmate's attraction points will be represented by the fingertips on your left hand.

The fingertips represent attraction points for both the male and the female. There are no set guidelines on what those attraction points will be as all of us are made differently, and what may be an attraction that I desire might be different for another guy, and the same holds for the woman's side.

The chart below shows my five personal attraction points and how I would place them. I always use the thumb as my starting point and will explain why later.

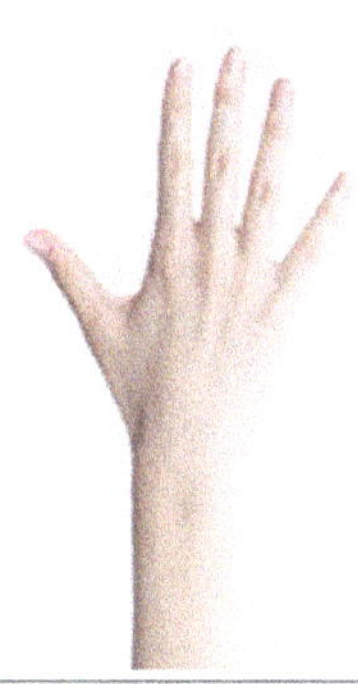

Attraction Points:

Little Finger- Sweet sounding voice

Next finger – Attractive Face

Middle Finger – Shapely Body

Index Finger – Eyes that Sparkle

Thumb – Beautiful Smile

Attractions DO NOT connect!!!

Relationships built on attractions alone are easily broken, but those that search the invisible qualities of soul for the fruits of the Spirit and find them, then they have a bond they can lock onto that will last forever.

The smile plays a significant role in an initial attraction. A smile is somewhat a reflection of the soul. A happy smile is not just sexy; although it can be part of a sexual allure, it is more linked to the spirit's condition, which is extremely important in building a long-term relationship. A happy spirit means the person is more in sync with God than with the world and all its distractions, including the attraction to the physical things in life.

An additional part of the smile qualifier would be for that smile to have nice "teeth" and nice "lips" that I would desire to look at and kiss every day for the rest of my life. A good kiss communicates deeply into the spirit of your soulmate and lets them know you are truly connected with them. I explain the kiss more deeply when I reveal how to fulfill all five of your soulmate's love languages in one setting.

The second important attraction feature for me is the eyes, another great communicator of the soul! I focus on seeking a deep spiritual connection, so I aim to look at every feature that might give me a peek into their soul. I have heard it said that when a spirit is deeply connected to God, the eyes will have a special sparkle reflecting the light of God. Eyes can also reflect hurt, rejection, and despair. God instructed me to look deep into the eyes. If I could see the light through them, a door would open for a deeper search of her soul, enabling a transition from the attraction phase to the connection phase.

My third attraction point was a shapely body. I was not looking for a perfect model-bodied woman. I just wanted someone who looks good, is active, and could play sports with me for all the good days I have left (I hope many, but only God knows). Unfortunately, our bodies change as no one is exempted from aging. I am sorry to inform you, invincible folks, but we all grow old (if we are blessed) and die!

I count my blessings of being able to play sports in my old age as a wonderful gift from God. I enjoy pickleball, golf, cycling, and anything that I have the energy to enjoy. At 76, I feel blessed every morning when I wake up and can get out of bed and play pickleball for two or three hours (and sometimes longer). I thank God for my physical health and mobility every day. Having a soulmate who can be as active and enjoy sports as I am is important in selecting the body shape and condition.

My fourth attraction feature is an attractive face. We are all designed with different perceptions of beauty. When I see a photo or meet a potential soulmate, I ask myself if this is a face I would enjoy looking at every morning for the rest of my life. The attraction feature does not entice me if I cannot say yes. Ultimately, that face will change over time as we age, but so will the depth of your love that teaches you beauty is not just skin deep; it goes far below the skin and deep into the spirit.

My fifth attraction point is a sweet-sounding voice. Upon my first encounter with a soulmate, I question myself if that's the voice I want to listen to for the rest of my life. There's a strong possibility that, over time, constantly listening to numerous voices could become overwhelming. That's why a sweet voice is an important attraction point for me.

I believe these five attraction features are attached to the fingertips of my right hand. So I then bring my fingertips together from my right hand, which indicate my five attraction points, and I connect them to the fingers of my potential soulmate. It signals both of us that we are attracted to each other.

If you are deeply attracted, press hard on your fingertips to demonstrate a very extensive attraction. But then, please notice how easy it is to pull your fingertips away, as there is no solid or interlocking "connection" between the two.

As stated earlier, these are attraction points. So, as a male, if you took the fingertips of your right hand and placed them against the fingertips of your left hand, which represents your future soulmate and her attraction points, you will note that you are touching but not connected, you can easily pull them apart. There is no real connection that ties them together. That clearly communicates that a relationship built upon attraction could not create a bond that would last till death do you part.

Many men and women give into the physical desires of their dating partner, thinking it will create a deeper bond. However, it would be a gross error in judgment for a man or woman to try to establish a lasting relationship just on an attraction leading to sex. Having sex with someone you are attracted to, thinking it will help the relationship to become solid and last, is a very false and unwise premise for building a lasting relationship.

Sex does not form a bond; it satisfies the lust of the eye. Proverbs 31:30: "Charm is deceptive, and beauty is fleeting; but a woman who fears the Lord is to be praised. James 1:11: "For the sun rises with scorching heat and withers the plant; its blossom falls, and its beauty is destroyed. In the same way, the rich will fade away even while they go about their business."

Many women and men have been fooled, thinking that giving of themselves to their mate will entice their mate to want them and love them more.

Love is not a physical attraction or a sexual encounter. Both factors play a part in a relationship, but love that creates a long-term bond is only established through a clear understanding of what God is bringing together in a marriage. Matthew 19:4-6 "Have you not read that he who created them from the beginning made them male and female, and said, 'Therefore a man shall leave his father and his mother and hold fast to his wife, and the two shall become one flesh?' So they are no longer two but one flesh." Therefore, what God has joined together, let no one separate.

We know God does not mean two bodies will physically become one because God is not concerned about the flesh. Ecclesiastes 5:15: "Everyone comes naked from their mother's womb, and as everyone comes, so they depart. They take nothing from their toil that they can carry in their hands." Isaiah 44:2: "This is what the Lord says— he who made you, who formed you in the womb, and who will help you: Do not be afraid, Jacob, my servant, Jeshurun, whom I have chosen." We are made in his likeness through our spiritual being, not our flesh. Isaiah 44:24: "This is what the Lord says— your Redeemer, who formed you in the womb: I am the Lord, the Maker of all things, who stretches out the heavens, who spreads out the earth by myself."

God makes it clear to us in Jeremiah that he has a plan for our lives before we are ever put into our mother's womb. Jeremiah 1:5: "Before I formed you in the womb I knew you, before you were born, I set you apart; I appointed you as a prophet to the nations."

Again, God is not referring to the physical bodies; and he is clearly referring to our spirit. It is the spirit that can be united with another soul, and the two become one spirit in purpose, and that purpose is to serve God. So how do we go from the physical attraction to a spiritual connection that can eventually create that bond of becoming one that God refers to in his word?

Let's look at how Peter describes that inner being in 1 Peter 3:2-4: "When they see the purity and reverence of your lives. Your beauty should not come from outward adornment, such as elaborate hairstyles and the wearing of gold jewelry or fine clothes. Rather, it should be that of your inner self, the unfading beauty of a gentle and quiet spirit, which is of great worth in God's sight."

It is the spirit that is worthy before God. So, how do we seek the right spirit to establish the connection God wants to form between a man and a woman? We will discover that in our next chapter, where we will learn how to establish connection and bonding. It begins with a clear understanding of Romans 7:22: "For in my inner being I delight in God's law."

Chapter 7 - The Connection and Bonding

The connection phase is critical in establishing a solid relationship with your future soulmate and God. Knowing what you seek is essential for the relationship if you strongly feel attracted enough to someone and desire to talk with a potential soulmate. This clarity helps the relationship mature into a meaningful and lasting bond. In the Hands of Love, God told me, "To find the right soulmate, you must evaluate the soul's invisible or unseen qualities." He suggested the invisible qualities or fruits of the spirit could be explained using the four empty spaces between the fingers.

First, let me remind you that you are looking at or evaluating the presence of the invisible qualities of another person's soul. And how would we see the invisible? Through the powerful spirit God has given us. 2 Corinthians 4:18: "So we fix our eyes not on what is seen, but on what is unseen, since what is seen is temporary, but what is unseen is eternal."

The physical qualities of a person are temporary, but the spiritual qualities are eternal. God has given us the miraculous power through the Holy Spirit to read spirits. He tells us to test spirits in 1 John 4:1: "Dear friends, do not believe every spirit, but test the spirits to see whether they are from God, because many false prophets have gone out into the world." God would not tell us to do something impossible for us to do, and he has provided us with the ability to test spirits.

Holiness is our goal; to be holy is a prerequisite for being God's reflection. Romans 6:22: "But now that you have been set free from sin and have become slaves of God, the benefit you reap leads to holiness, and the result is eternal life."

In his holy word, God speaks of the gifts of the Holy Spirit and tells us that the spirit has nine fruits. "But the fruit of the Spirit is love, joy, peace, forbearance, kindness, goodness, faithfulness, gentleness and self-control." (Galatians 5:22-23)

God wants us to be a mirror that reflects the light of love. Our adoption and growth in the nine fruits of the Holy Spirit will make us become more like God—adopt his virtues and not act like God. When these elements are present in our soul, they send a very positive light into the world and into the heart of our soulmate, a door to allow the two to become one with God.

God desires that we all connect and bond with him so that he can transform us into servants' hearts like his son, Jesus Christ. He desires that we grow and mature in the nine fruits of the Holy Spirit, and when we do, our lives will be fit to bond with God and our soulmates.

God intentionally identifies and emphasizes nine specific qualities given to us by the Holy Spirit, which help us grow and mature in our walk with him. These nine fruits are major fruits and qualities that come directly from God—himself—and every practicing Christian should strive to fully develop the nine fruits of spirit within their personality, seeking maturity in their faith to deepen their connection with God and their soulmate.

To help our readers better understand God's building block approach, let us review and explore the nine specific fruits to know how each reflects our growth and maturity in our walk with God.

After that, we will view the Scripture verse indicating where these nine fruits come from and then present a brief commentary on each of these fruits to understand what each is all about.

To begin with, these fruits possess powers that can dramatically change the quality of your life and well-being if you allow the Holy Spirit to lead and work all nine into your personality.

"But the fruit of the Spirit is love, joy, peace, forbearance, kindness, goodness, faithfulness, gentleness and self-control" (Galatians 5:22-23)

Here are the nine fruits of the Holy Spirit listed in the order that God established. Love is the first fruit because God is love. You can never mature in the other fruits of the spirit if God, or love, is not present.

These nine fruits are beautiful when grown in one's spirit. Note here: I did not say perfect, as none of us are perfect.

1. Love (Greek: Agape)

Love is often considered the highest and most essential virtue. It refers to unconditional love, modeled by God's love for humanity. God's love is about selfless care and concern for others. Does this person you are considering as a soulmate show love to everyone, or are they selective? God's unconditional love is unconditional; he loves everyone because he created everyone.

Scriptures:

John 15:13: "Greater love has no one than this: to lay down one's life for one's friends."

1 Corinthians 13:4-7: "Love is patient, love is kind... It always protects, always trusts, always hopes, always perseveres."

2. Joy (Greek: Chara)

Joy goes beyond mere happiness and is a deep, abiding sense of well-being stemming from a relationship with God and his precious Love. It results from living in harmony with God and finding fulfillment in his presence. Can you see an unflappable spirit that keeps you joyful even in tough times?

Scriptures:

Nehemiah 8:10: "The joy of the Lord is your strength."

John 15:11: "I have told you this so that my joy may be in you and that your joy may be complete."

3. Peace (Greek: Eirene)

This fruit refers to inner tranquility and calmness, even in difficult situations. It is about being content with life and trusting in God's control, offering freedom from anxiety and worry. The peace of a deeply attached spirit to God will always reflect calm, for it does not worry.

Scriptures:

John 14:27: "Peace I leave with you; my peace I give you."

Philippians 4:7: "And the peace of God, which transcends all understanding, will guard your hearts and your minds in Christ Jesus."

4. Patience (Long-suffering) (Greek: Makrothumia)

Patience involves endurance and tolerance, which delay suffering without becoming upset. It's about maintaining a spirit of calm and gentleness in the face of adversity or provocation. This quality is key to the spiritual growth of all the remaining fruits of the spirit.

Scriptures:

Colossians 3:12: "Therefore, as God's chosen people... clothe yourselves with compassion, kindness, humility, gentleness and patience."

James 1:3-4: "The testing of your faith produces perseverance. Let perseverance finish its work so that you may be mature and complete."

5. Kindness (Greek: Chrestotes)

It refers to being considerate, compassionate, and generous toward others. Kindness reflects God's goodness and shows concern for the well-being of others. Kindness is the by-product of facing trials, where you thank God for his help and love others as he has loved you.

Scriptures:

Ephesians 4:32: "Be kind and compassionate to one another, forgiving each other, just as in Christ God forgave you."

Titus 3:4-5: "But when the kindness and love of God our Savior appeared, he saved us."

6. Goodness (Greek: Agathosune)

Goodness involves moral integrity and striving for righteousness. It's about doing what is right, fair, and just in all situations, aligning with God's ethical standards. Goodness is the actions you show to others as you seek to show God your appreciation for his goodness.

Scriptures:

Psalm 23:6: "Surely your goodness and love will follow me all the days of my life."

Romans 12:21: "Do not be overcome by evil, but overcome evil with good."

7. Faithfulness (Greek: Pistis)

It refers to loyalty, trustworthiness, and a commitment to remain faithful to one's promises and beliefs. It involves being dependable and steadfast in relationships with God and others.

Scriptures:

Lamentations 3:22-23: "Because of the Lord's great love we are not consumed... Great is your faithfulness."

Proverbs 3:3-4: "Let love and faithfulness never leave you... Then you will win favor and a good name in the sight of God and man."

8. Gentleness (or Meekness) (Greek: Prautes)

Gentleness is about being humble and mild-mannered. It does not imply weakness but rather strength under control. It means respecting others' feelings and treating people with care and respect. Being gentle is an excellent sign of a mature spirit.

Scriptures:

Matthew 5:5: "Blessed are the meek, for they will inherit the earth."

1 Peter 3:15: "But in your hearts revere Christ as Lord... do this with gentleness and respect."

9. Self-Control (Greek: Egkrateia)

Self-control is exercising restraint over one's desires, emotions, and actions. It helps individuals resist temptations and live according to

God's commandments rather than being driven by impulses. This quality assures you that this spirit is deeply connected to God.

Scriptures:

Proverbs 25:28: "Like a city whose walls are broken through is a person who lacks self-control."

1 Corinthians 9:25: "Everyone who competes in the games goes into strict training... to get a crown that will last forever."

Reflection:

These nine fruits collectively represent a person's character led by the Holy Spirit/God, the Father. The presence of these virtues in a believer's life is evidence of spiritual growth and transformation. They are not traits that people naturally exhibit all the time but are cultivated through a relationship with God and the empowering work of the Holy Spirit.

The fruits of the spirit serve as a guide for Christian behavior and a reflection of Christ-like living. They encourage believers to pursue a life grounded in love, peace, kindness, and self-discipline, showing God's love to the world through their actions and attitudes. Before we discuss each of these nine fruits in further detail, note the following:

The word "spirit" means the nine fruits that come directly from the Holy Spirit, and we mature in them as we grow.

As we grow in God's love, peace, joy, and goodness, like a computer program, all these will be automatically downloaded into our spirit and help us grow. These divine personality traits and qualities of God are transmitted into the core of our personality to facilitate our maturing.

Think about what this means. God, the Father and Creator, allows us to share a part of his divine nature by connecting us with his Holy Spirit and receiving these nine divine, life-changing, invisible qualities directly into our souls and personalities!

God, the Father, explicitly tells us in this verse that these nine fruits come directly from his Holy Spirit. It takes maturity and a deep connection with God to appreciate the magnitude of such an experience.

So, how do we get that deep connection with Jesus to bear fruit? Jesus tells us in the Great Commission: Matthew 28:18-20 (NIV): "Then Jesus came to them and said, "All authority in heaven and on earth has been given to me. 19 Therefore go and make disciples of all nations, baptizing them in the name of the Father and of the Son and of the **Holy Spirit,** and teaching them to obey everything I have commanded you. And surely, I am with you always, to the very end of the age."

WE must seek the truth of God's word to obey it and mature into the Spiritual Vine that can produce fruit.

How can we put that into practicality? Let's see!

When dating, be open and discuss your relationships with your friends, especially those who follow Christianity. Sometimes, the feedback you get is exactly what you need. When you hide information about your dates and your new dating partner, you could be hiding Satan in a closet. Have no closets where God can't get in, please. If you can't be open about your relationship, there is probably something wrong you are not seeing or denying.

Jesus tells us that he is the vine, and we are the branches. John 15: "I am the vine; you are the branches. If you remain in me and I in you, you will bear much fruit; apart from me you can do nothing." The branches draw their life from the vine, not vice versa. And just like that, we also draw our life directly from Jesus. Jesus releases his divine life directly into us through the Holy Spirit, like the vine will release the tree's life into the branches.

In one short but compelling Scripture verse, God, the Father, gives us an incredible revelation on what can go on behind the scenes in the spiritual realm for those willing to work with him in this sanctification process. Sanctification is the process of becoming more like Christ; it is a lifelong journey in which the Holy Spirit helps us overcome the desires of the flesh.

Look at the chart below that associates the invisible qualities of the fruits of the spirit with the specific areas of the hand that I call valleys. There are three fruits of the spirit in the big valley and two in the other three valleys.

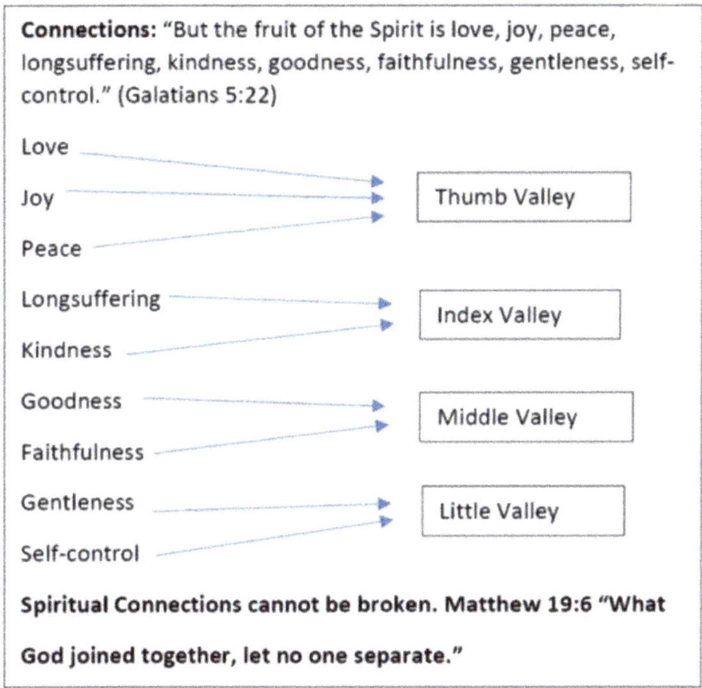

Imagine you are now with your new soulmate, and you have shared your five attraction features, allowed your fingertips to meet, and pressed hard to show a deep attraction to each other. Now, take the most essential step in establishing your relationship: slide your fingertips over to the empty spaces and discuss each fruit of the spirit individually.

Start in the big valley, where love, joy, and peace reside. These three are the building blocks. They give you the strength to deal with trials or sufferings. When you count your trials as a blessing, you develop a humble spirit that leads to a kind heart. A kind heart cultivates good works and fosters a more faithful spirit. The closer you walk with God, the more gentle your spirit will become. Once you have matured and consistently displayed gentleness, you will have a spirit that has a mature, disciplined connection with God, the Father, and you will produce good fruit and be a great soulmate.

Now, go deeply into the valleys with your fingers until your palms touch. That indicates you are both mature in all the fruits of the spirit and a good match for your soulmate.

Now lock your fingers on the back of your partner's hand and notice that you cannot pull the connection apart. You have a solid connection built on along with the invisible qualities of the Holy Spirit God instilled in you.

Now close your thumbs over your index finger; that is God's seal for the relationship.

As you analyze each fruit in each valley and see that your soulmate is deeply rooted in each one, you have what it takes to create a solid connection that will bless each of you.

Remember that all these fruits are aligned in a progressive pattern for growth where love is the building block of them all. The more ingrained these qualities mature in you; the more prepared you are for being an eternal soulmate to the person God brings into your path. The final quality of having a mature spirit is self-control; when walking so close to God, you are a bright, shining light into the world everywhere you go.

The Bonding Phase

Matthew 19:6: "What God joined together, let no one separate."

If you have completed the connection phase of the relationship, then you are now postured to establish a bond that will last for eternity. When you have completed a deep search of all the fruits of the spirit, and your palms have drawn closer together where they are touching, you can now lock your fingers over the other person's hand, and you will note that you can no longer pull away. A spiritual connection works similarly; it is a deep connection. It will allow you to create a bond that can endure all things and last forever. Even after death, it lasts for eternity.

The Pinnacle of Life

When the fruits of the spirit are correctly aligned, and you seek to improve your walk with God, the pyramid of life Best explains your walk together.

How do you build a pyramid to explain how the power of God works in your life? You start one day at a time and work your way to the top. The pinnacle is heaven, but we climb the mountain one day at a time.

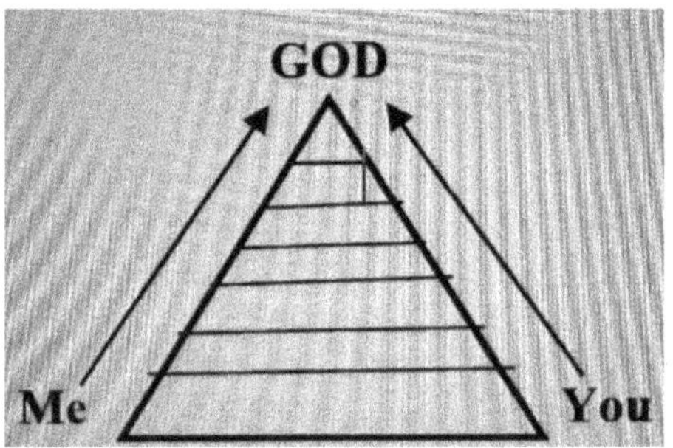

When two soulmates are both pursuing the top of the pyramid to get closer to God, you will notice that the closer they get to God, the smaller the space between them gets, and they grow closer and closer to each other. Our goal is to grow closer to God daily so that when we depart this world, we will be ready to meet Jesus face-to-face and begin our eternal journey. It only takes one to go the opposite way to create a massive gap in a relationship. That is why we must search to find that similar spirit. Eternal-bound soulmates send much of God's light into the world of darkness.

Chapter 8 - The Hands of Love Process

Let me begin by saying God is amazing! I had an excellent soulmate for 49 years, and I did not want to seem selfish and ask God for another fantastic soulmate. I staunchly believe that it would seem too self-seeking of me, but eventually, God knew what was in my heart, and thus, he far exceeded my expectations when he brought my new wife into my life.

After a year of searching, I wondered if I would ever find anyone with the good looks and spiritual qualities to match the desires of my heart. It was going to take a very special lady. It appeared that finding a woman seasoned or mature in all nine fruits of the spirit, which I knew was necessary to create the God-designed spiritual bond, would be a rare find and much of a hustle. In my mind, it was going to take a miracle from God. Oh, yeah, I almost forgot that his business is performing daily miracles! So, let me share my second and glorious miracle, my latest God story, with you.

The Hands of Love

One day when I was dreaming,

God, said open up your hands

He said spread your fingers far apart

and let me help you understand.

The Hands are good for doing many things

They are Good for serving others and wearing golden rings

But let my spirit teach you how to let them be your guide

If you listen to what I teach you

they will lead you to the perfect bride.

The hands of love were inspired by my precious God above.

He is my creator, so I trust Him to lead me to my perfect love.

The hands of love will guide me, they led me to you

And there could not be a better match for me

For God spoke to my spirit and said this is very true

God said your fingertips are attraction points that opens up a door

But lasting relationships can't rest there, they require a whole lot more

The invisible qualities of the soul make lasting relationships for you and me

So, take your time to study these and you will truly see

God lets you name your five attraction points as you see fit to do

But He will guide you through the invisible valleys to find the success He has planned for you

Between your thumb and index finger lies the big valley of love, joy and peace,

They are the root of all the fruits of the spirit that without them life's bonds will cease.

Love for God must be present for a relationship to grow.

God's Love will produce a joy that will clearly send a glow.

The joy leads to peace that comes from knowing and trusting God

That peace will bless you through all of life wherever you may trod

The next valley over lies the long suffering that we all will face

But kindness is the reward we gain from being steady in God's love and grace.

In the next valley over lies Goodness and Faithfulness that come from knowing and trusting God

When one's life reflects these fruits, their spirit shows the power by God's accepting nod

The invisible fruits of the spirit in the last valley are gentleness and self-control

These two qualities reflect maturity and a spirit that will help others to grow.

When searching for a soulmate if you seek these special traits above all

God will bless your pathway with a bond that cannot be broken because you have accepted His call.

My second wife and I first met at the online dating site Christian Café. Initially, we had a few exchanges; however, I quickly offered my number to text and talk soon and take whatever was brewing between us a step ahead. Things went quite well, and we quickly realized something special was occurring between us. It seemed more than a good fit, and the more we talked, the better it got.

We shared the paths our lives had been down over the past couple of years before our meeting. We were amazed to see how God had directed our steps. He directed our steps from different parts of the world to allow our paths to cross and for us to meet. When we reviewed that all, we could see God's miracle-working hands that had weaved our paths together, and that miracle became the impetus for sharing the "Hands of Love" inspiration I received from God.

She was far more refreshing to my soul than what I could ever have imaged that God could find for me. Looking back on my first love and how well that worked out, I felt ashamed to sell God short. He amazed me again! After all, he is all-knowing and all-powerful and knows my spirit better than I do since he created it and can make anything happen. Shame on me! So, let me give you a few details in this great "Hands of Love" God story.

It was her cute hat pose that drew my attention. Even though she was living too far north, I was hoping she might be open to moving to

Sunny Florida. After all, nobody leaves Florida to move to the cold north. I think half of northern states lives in Florida during the winter months! We call them "snowbirds!"

Her curious but confident look made me want to stop and read her profile. The problem was that she was north of my Old Kentucky Home, and I was in Florida. So I knew it would be a stretch to hope she would be open to moving. But a thought struck me: my first soulmate was from the northern state of Ohio, and that worked out really well for me, so maybe God wants me to search that far north again! So, I decided to give it a look and just see where it goes.

I sent her a message you can read as I have cut and pasted our initial conversations. You can see I went by the name "TopGunDave." I was an Air Weapons Controller in the Air Force, and once assigned to a Top Gun Squadron called the Aggressors. My new title is related to being a Top Gun for God. I knew this name would be a magnet for the right person and a turnoff to those not deeply connected with God. She went by an alias name.

After reading her profile what really attracted me to her was her interpretation of Psalm 139:14. Her very deep descriptive expressions of that verse told me she had deep spiritual roots worthy of my pursuit. I was really moved when I read her reflection on the verse, "to be made in God's image, and the boundless grace and promise of what that means." That clearly communicated that her connection with God was deep, precisely what my soul sought to find.

She beautifully described the verse as "simultaneously a celebration and worship of our Lord's divine love, and it's also a summons to live guided by scripture and in accordance with Christ's teachings and the path he lays."

My heart sank. She clearly communicated to me that she desired to have the word of God and Christ as the guide of her life. That warmed my heart and reinforced that there was a really good reason God had directed me to look deeper into her profile, the cute northern girl with the hat!

Needless to say, her words sounded like music to my ears, so I was more than anxious to talk with her to validate the sincerity of her writings. But I cautiously repeat my position stated earlier: people can cut and paste sweet words, so it is not until you can talk with them that you will really know if they truly represent who they claim to be; for me, that is a faithful follower of Jesus.

Here are a few screenshots showing some of our initial communications, which I started on January 24th, and her first response on January 30th.

I was disappointed that it took her six days to respond.

Original Message (Sent Jan 24, 12:12 PM)

Walking with God means we accept the premise of Proverbs 16:9, In his heart a man will plan his course, but the Lord will direct his steps. When God leads me to a path where my footprints cross with someone special like you, I attempt to open the door to confirm if this is where God is truly leading me. The spirit speaks quickly and soon we know if this is a real spiritual connection God is working, or if it was just our own curiosity. So, lets open the door to see if this beautiful spiritual lady is a potential match for a real Top Gun for God! If you would like to talk, send me a text and I will call you. My cell is: 352-267-5611. I hope you like Florida!!!! Be blessed, Dave

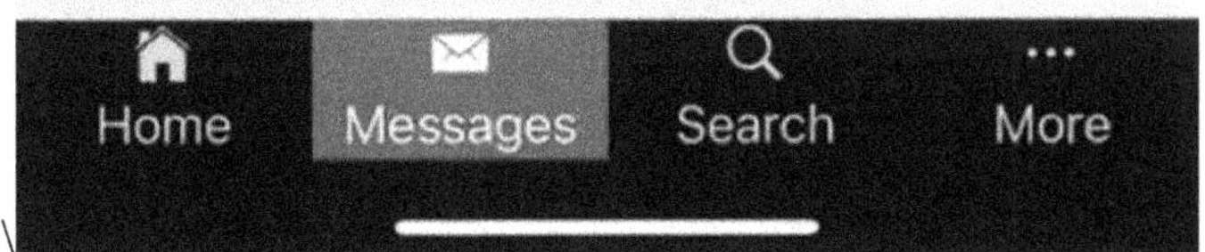

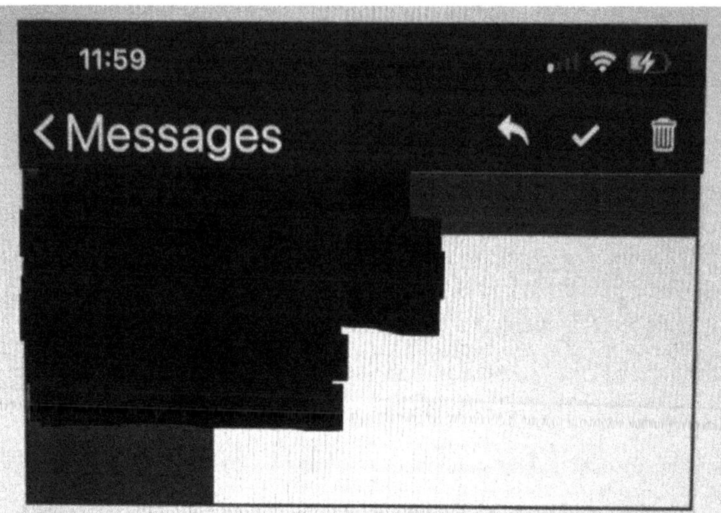
11:59
< Messages
RE: Life's Pathway
Jan 30, 2022
Thank you for the beautiful invitation,
which is touching and does a woman
honor. Your words and reflections
about faith and life and relationships
are truly beacons

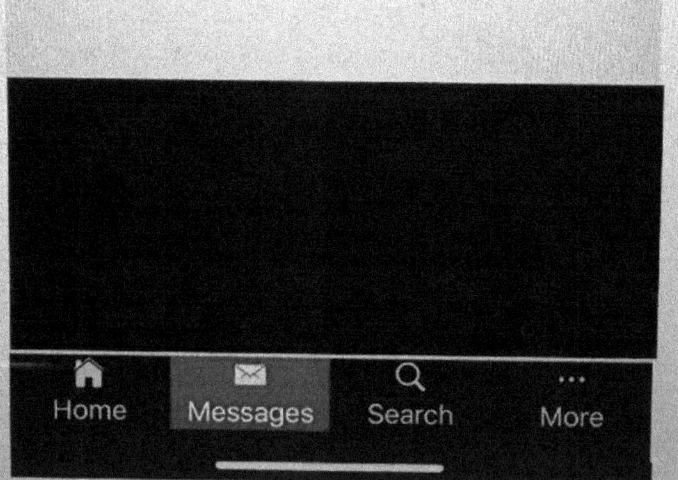
Home   Messages   Search   More

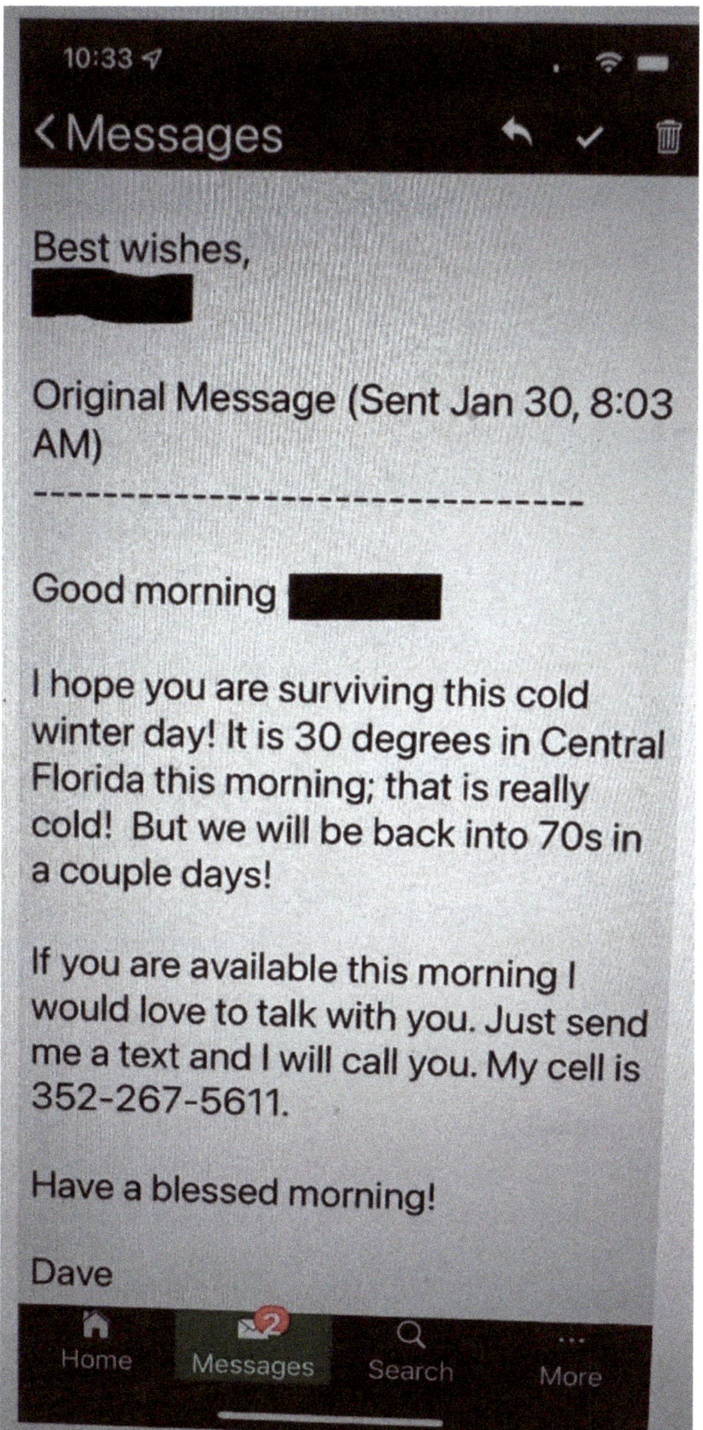

10:33

< Messages

Best wishes,

Original Message (Sent Jan 30, 8:03 AM)

Good morning

I hope you are surviving this cold winter day! It is 30 degrees in Central Florida this morning; that is really cold! But we will be back into 70s in a couple days!

If you are available this morning I would love to talk with you. Just send me a text and I will call you. My cell is 352-267-5611.

Have a blessed morning!

Dave

Home   Messages   Search   More

February 1, 2022

Good Morning!

I look forward to talking with you. You are pretty far north so you do get a lot colder there than we do in Central Florida!!

I play Pickleball from 7:00am to 10:30am, so I will be free to talk after that.

Thanks for your response.

Be blessed,

Dave

When someone has not posted recent photos, you should not feel bad to ask them to send some recent ones. The exchange of photos is a crucial step to see if the person will be transparent with you. Many people like to show you how they looked when they were younger. I always tried just to show photos taken within the last six months. No one wants to be surprised when they meet a potential soulmate by discovering they are 10 years older than their photos.

Also, if they become too transparent and send photos showing more than they should, their spirit is not in the right place to establish a pure Christian bond. Photo exchanges need to be open and transparent about how you look today but not to entice someone with sexy photos that you might find in porn magazines!

You will notice that I offered my cell phone up front so she could text me, and hopefully, we could begin talking as soon as possible. You might ask, what is wrong with texting for a while? My answer is simple but very clear: first, I like to hear their voice to determine if she has a voice that I could listen to for the rest of my life.

Secondly, spirits can better connect when talking as compared to texting. When you speak with someone, you can sense if the fruits of the spirit are present. The conversation flows from the spirit with what it carries. The truth is transmitted and not the mere, unmeaningful words from a made-up script. Your spirit can sense the presence of the invisible qualities of joy, peace, love, patience, and all the other five. Matthew 15:18: "But the things that come out of a person's mouth come from the heart, and these defile them." Text messages are not from the heart. People can copy them from someone else or rewrite them well, which means they can be deceptive. The spoken words, in contrast, come directly from the heart and, therefore, reveal who the person really is.

When we first talked, I immediately sensed a peaceful, loving, and joyful spirit. She was also learning about me and discovered that I was as accurate as my profile projected. I wanted to be upfront with her about what I was looking for, so I explained the Hands of Love concept in one of our talks. I went through every detail with her.

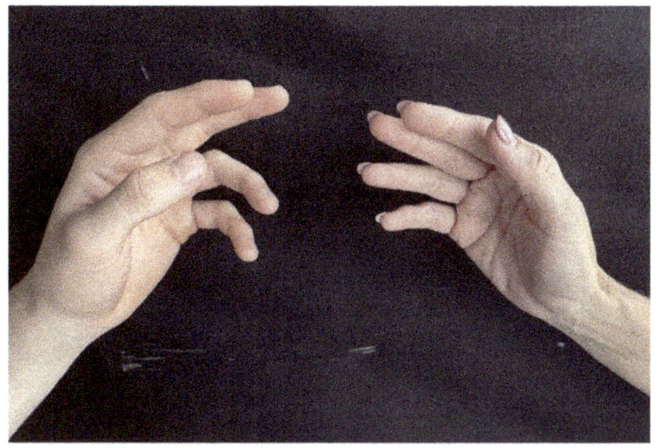

Photo of hands, fingertips facing each other but about 3" apart, signifying a first look that draws your attention

The first glance is our first look in person or a photo, creating a drawing and making us want to get closer to each other. It could be a church setting, or a visit with a friend, just out shopping, or an online website where we met.

As you move closer to validate the attraction, you just hope it is mutual.

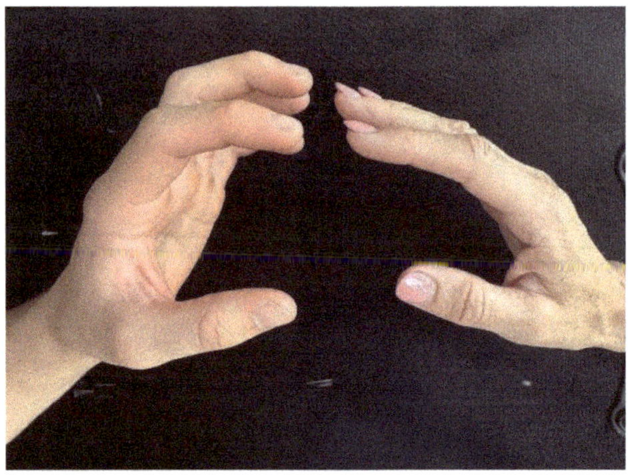

Photo of hands, fingertips coming close together, signifying attraction and interest in a first meeting to allow the spirits to interact.

Then I had her hold her hands up and bring her fingertips together and I described my five attractions and asked her to do the same.

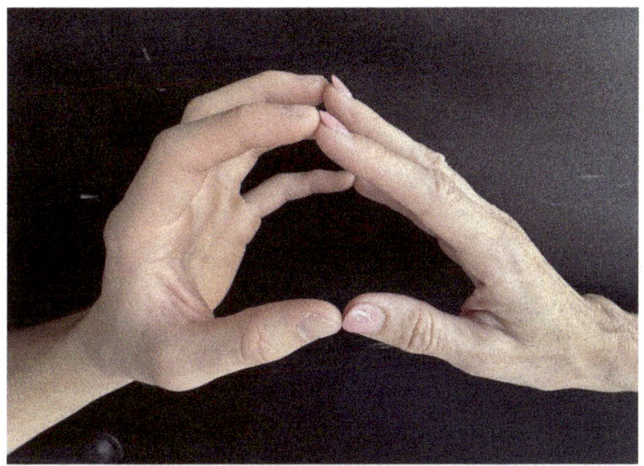

Photo of hands, fingertips coming together, but barley touching, signifying the attraction points are confirmed and a first meeting set to allow the spirits to interact.

Attraction Points:

Little Finger- Sweet sounding voice

Next finger – Attractive Face

Middle Finger – Shapely Body

Index Finger – Eyes that Sparkle

Thumb – Beautiful Smile

Attractions DO NOT connect!!!

Then, I asked her to allow our fingertips to press against each other to demonstrate a profound attraction.

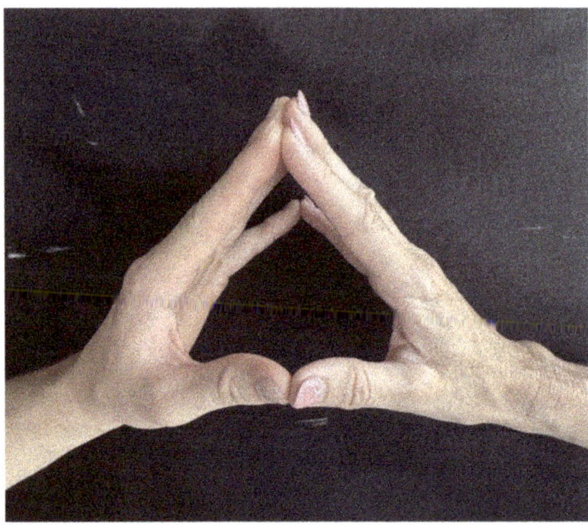

Photo of hands, fingertips pressing hard against each others, indicating a strong attraction

Then I pull my fingertips away and demonstrate for her how easy it was to separate from a relationship just built upon attractions.

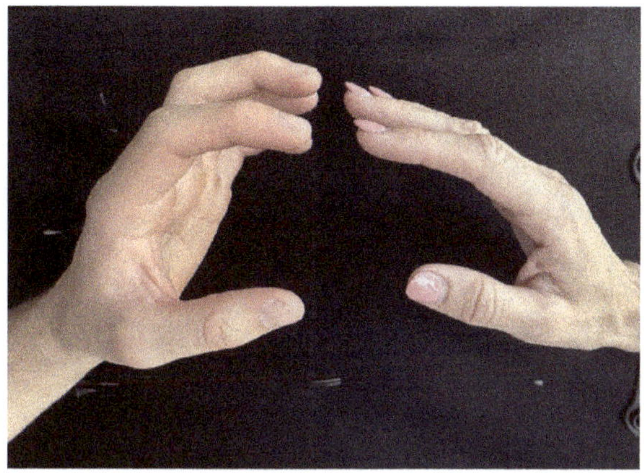

Photo of hands, her hand and fingertips still in place and my hand pulled away indicating that Attractions do not create a real Connection.

At this point I explain that long lasting relationships are not built upon attractions. God makes clear they are built upon our desire to draw unto him and for our spirits to seek the perfections of the "Fruits of the Spirit". So, God says, look at the invisible qualities of the soul, and if they possess deeply rooted fruits of the spirit, then you will find a soulmate. He said unto me, look at the empty spaces between the fingers, that is where you look for the invisible qualities of the soul that lead to a connection that is not easily broken.

Next, I explained the invisible qualities of the fruits of the spirit:

First Valley of Love: love, joy and peace, in the first space.

Then Second Valley of Love: long suffering and kindness.

The Third Valley of Love: goodness and faithfulness.

The Fourth Valley of Love: gentleness and self-control.

I explained how the success of the connection phase correlates to your soulmate's connection to God and the Fruits of the Spirit.

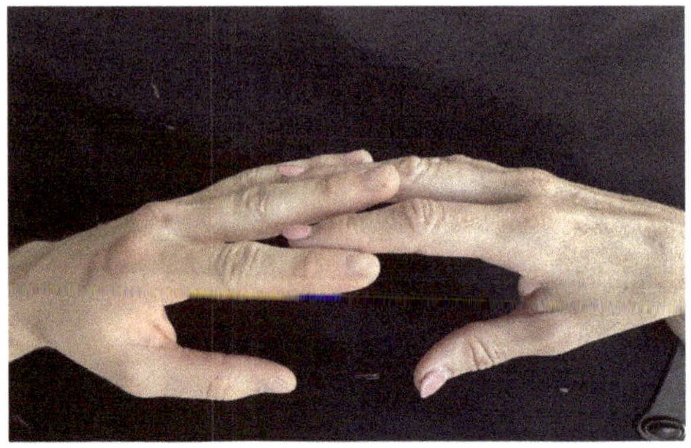

Photo of hands, the fingertips are now in the gaps ready to dive deep into the persons soul to see how deep the Fruits of the Spirit roots go. If they are only seen on occasion, the roots are not very deep.

I had her slide her fingers into the gaps between the fingers slowly and explained that this could take weeks or months to evaluate the depth of the fruits of the spirit in another person's soul. I told her that this slow process represented the time to discover the depth of the fruits of the spirit. I explained that someone can show early signs of being good, but after some time, they begin to show inconsistencies, and you know then that they are not as deeply rooted as they claimed. That is when you must evaluate whether this was God's plan or just your curiosity. It is best to move on if you feel it might be too hard to bring it together.

This is a very critical step as it takes time to validate the Fruits of the Spirit. It is easy to get excited when you "think" you have found the perfect soulmate, and you are anxious to get started. My word of caution is to give it time to ensure both parties have been totally transparent. Sometimes one can hide their faults in hopes of winning you over, only to reveal their true self after you have tied the knot. Then the opportunity to end the relationship becomes much more difficult.

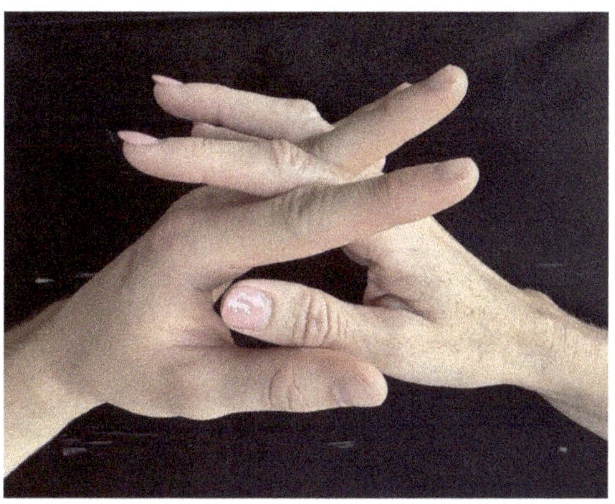

Photo of hands, her hand and fingertips are gone deep and found good roots. We are now so close our palms are touching, and our fingers can lock on creating a solid Connection

I explained to my new soulmate that you should seek a relationship where the deeper you search, the better it gets, and eventually, your palms are touching. You can now lower your fingers, lock on, and create a solid connection, an image of a locked relationship that cannot be broken. That is God's desire for every marriage.

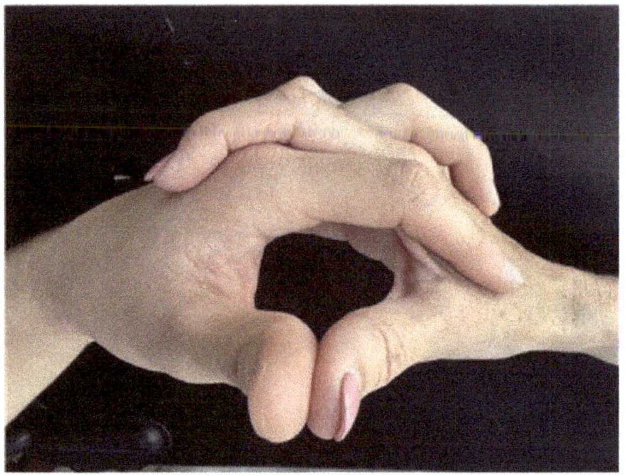

That is when your palms can touch, and your fingers can lock on which symbolizes you have a connected relationship that God can bless. As per Matthew 19:6: "So they are no longer two, but one flesh. Therefore, what God has joined together, let no one separate."

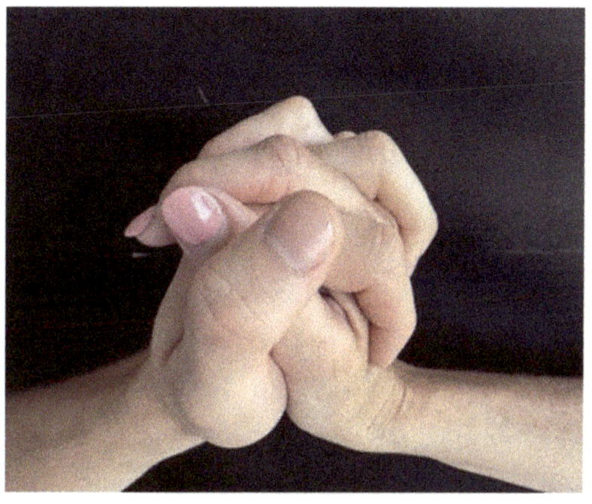

Photo of hands, both thumbs close over top of the index finger indicating God's sealing of the marriage creating a Bond for life.

She was all in, so we began talking daily and started praying together very soon. After two months of talking, praying, and connecting the best we could, our spirits had reached a point of fulfillment, and we needed to meet. She had enough of the cold north weather and volunteered to fly down to Florida to meet me.

I could only say that God spoke to her heart and gave her the courage and comfort to meet a guy she only knew from a website and two months of phone calls because it was precarious, yet she felt no fear. That is until she arrived at the airport, and then Satan started putting doubt in her mind, like filling her mind with questions: "What are you doing? You do not know this guy. He could be a mass murderer!" and whatnot.

Satan was trying to divert her from the confidence God had placed in her spirit, and he was attempting to turn her away from God's plan for her future. She was talking to her mom on the phone, who was also sending her alerts, but then she saw me, and God performed his miracle and calmed her spirit. When she made eye contact with me, her spirit knew I was a man of God. We had many discussions about our faith, so addressing our expectations for first-impression attraction was next on our list. We met, and she felt secure, so our spirits connected, and God took over, and Satan beat feet. From that moment forward we both felt that God had brought us together as our spirits felt a special delight in being with each other.

Our engagement occurred on her third visit during my home Bible study. That day, I was teaching my fellow Christians how to be a Top Gun for God! At the end of the lesson, I put the Top Gun video on the big screen with the "Take My Breath Away" song playing. I left the room, put on my flight jacket, grabbed my helmet, and walked back in. The members of my Bible study group knew what was about to happen. She was laughing as I strutted around the room until I got down on my knee and pulled the ring out of my pocket, and I "took her breath away!" She said yes, so we hugged each other, and then I had planned a special dance.

So we went to the Florida Room, and I played Anne Murray's song, "Could I Have This Dance!" And we danced! It was a very special night I will never forget, and I would try to repeat it often.

I expected a "YES", so I had a cake prepared!!!

Shortly thereafter, I introduced her to the "Five Love Languages" and how we should seek to fulfill each other's needs. Let me give a brief synopsis if you have not heard of that.

Baptist Pastor Gary Chapman 1992 described the Five Love Languages as crucial to keeping your soulmate happy. The Five Love Languages describe expressing a heartfelt commitment to your mate. It outlines five general ways romantic partners express and experience love, which Chapman calls "love languages."

1. Words of Affirmation

2. Quality Time

3. Gifts

4. Acts of Service

5. Physical Touching

Learning these love languages will get your marriage off to a great start or enhance a long-standing one! Chapman explains in his book the purpose of each "language" and how to identify the one that has the most meaning to your spouse. WE all have shifts in our lives, so there may be a change in which one might mean the most for today.

What I did for her was something I would recommend to every man to do regularly for his spouse. I demonstrated all five Love Languages in 10 minutes.

1. I told her, "Wife to be, my love, as an 'ACT OF SERVICE,' let me offer you the best seat in the house; come and sit on my comfy lap."

2. As she sits on your lap, put your arms around her and fulfill her "needs of TOUCHING." As you hug her, rub any part of her body that you know will make her feel your love.

3. Now you offer her a very special "GIFT." You give her the greatest gift: a passionate kiss that allows her to feel a real connection.

4. You hold that kiss for a while and then gently pull away with this "WORD OF AFFIRMATION;" "That was the best kiss of my life. Could we do it every day?"

5. Then tell her how you will give her all the QUALITY TIME; she wants to repeat the fulfillment of her needs as many times as she wishes.

You have just made her day in ten minutes, and most likely, yours too.

WE were married on my dock, May 21, 2022, our wedding day was attended by my family, friends, and members of my home Bible study.

Our wedding was a wonderful experience, and my old dock recorded its second wedding, my favorite. The first dock wedding was with my neighbors, Brian and Tina, on April 20, 2008, but we were out of town at the time, so we missed it.

Our wedding day was wonderful and we felt very blessed. So, do you think Satan was happy and departed, and we rode off into the sunset and were delighted forever? Not a chance. He challenged us many times, and in many ways, but the fruits of the spirit were deeply rooted, and, like Top Guns for God, we wanted to win! Only God knows where it goes, he holds our future.

I could see that God was bringing people into our lives to assure us we were right where he wanted us to be. We both felt he directed us to get this book moving and published. He was leading me, and it was becoming very clear I needed to write. I was not sure, but God was!

Like everyone, we had a few bumps at the start of our marriage. I like to compare the use of the Japanese art of repairing a simple cracked bowl to the beauty of how God repairs us. In 15th-century Japanese Kintsugi art, a broken bowl with its shattered pieces symbolizes the scars of our lives. However, the bowl becomes even more beautiful when mended with gold.

Our trials become more beautiful when mended by Jesus, the maker of the gold. Through all our trials, we have proven to God that our love "connection" was a gift of God's leading. Our bond was deeply rooted in the "Fruits of the Spirit," we truly believed that we could do all things through Christ, including beating Satan in his attempts to destroy what God brought together. Psalm 119:143 (New International Version): "Trouble and distress have come upon me, but your commands give me delight."

I love my new wife increasingly every day, and I send her love devotionals every morning, and always end with, "Love You for Eternity!" One of her recent responses was so beautiful I feel the need to share it to show the beauty of her soul: "Good morning, my glorious songbird! How I long to hear your serenades up close and personal. I delight that our Lord made you and gave you to me… Have a blessed day, my Top Gun Dave (TGD). You are off to hit the courts, and I am off to hit the road! Love you bunches…" My response: **Thank you, God, for my Wife!**

God's plan for a successful marriage, as revealed through, God's word, the Bible, centers on:

- mutual love,
- respect,
- commitment,
- and spiritual growth.

Here are key principles that reflect God's design for a thriving marriage:

1. Love and Selflessness

Christ-like Love: God calls husbands to love their wives as Christ loved the church, willing to sacrifice and serve selflessly (Ephesians 5:25). Similarly, wives are called to love and respect their husbands.

Mutual Submission: Both spouses are to submit to one another out of reverence for Christ (Ephesians 5:21), prioritizing the needs and well-being of their partner over self-interest.

2. Unity and Oneness

Become One Flesh: In Genesis 2:24, God established marriage as a union where "a man leaves his father and mother and is united to his wife, and they become one flesh." This reflects emotional, physical, and spiritual intimacy that binds spouses together as one.

Partnership: Marriage is a covenant partnership, where each spouse supports the other through life's challenges and joys. God intended for marriage to be a team effort, where both partners complement one another's strengths and weaknesses (Ecclesiastes 4:9-12).

3. Faithfulness and Commitment

Lifelong Covenant: Marriage is a sacred, lifelong covenant before God. Jesus emphasized in Matthew 19:6, "What God has joined together, let no one separate," highlighting the permanence of this union.

Fidelity: Faithfulness to one another is a key part of God's plan. Hebrews 13:4 calls for marriage to be honored and protected, and infidelity to be avoided. Trust and commitment create the foundation for a secure, loving relationship.

4. Communication and Understanding

Listening and Speaking with Love: Proverbs 15:1 teaches that "a gentle answer turns away wrath," encouraging kind, thoughtful communication between spouses. Open, honest dialogue is essential for resolving conflicts, sharing emotions, and maintaining emotional intimacy.

Seek Understanding: 1 Peter 3:7 instructs husbands to live with their wives in an understanding way, reflecting a mutual desire to know and understand one another's needs, feelings, and perspectives. Each partner should seek to fulfill the Five Love Languages of their partner.

5. Forgiveness and Grace

Forgive One Another: Ephesians 4:32 teaches that forgiveness is crucial in any relationship, especially marriage. God's plan includes forgiving each other as Christ forgave us, allowing couples to heal, grow, and move past mistakes. Never allow past mistakes to arise and be inserted into new challenges, that is a very destructive model. Use Christ's example to forgive and forget. Hebrews 8:12 (NIV): "For I will forgive their wickedness and will remember their sins no more."

Grace in Imperfection: No spouse is perfect, and God's plan involves showing grace when imperfections surface. A successful marriage thrives on an attitude of grace, accepting each other's flaws while striving to grow together in Christ.

6. Spiritual Foundation

Christ at the Center: A successful marriage is rooted in a shared relationship with God. Ecclesiastes 4:12 says, "A cord of three strands is not easily broken," symbolizing the strength that comes when both husband and wife place Christ at the center of their union.

Prayer and Worship Together: Couples who pray together and seek God's guidance strengthen their spiritual bond. Colossians 3:16 encourages believers to teach, admonish, and sing spiritual songs together, which can enrich the spiritual life of a marriage. Become a part of a church family and allow your spirits to be interwoven with the spirits of God's family.

The giant sequoia (Sequoiadendron giganteum), one of the largest trees on Earth, has remarkable dimensions and a unique root system:

Height:

Giant sequoias can grow to an average height of 164 to 279 feet (50 to 85 meters), with some exceptional trees reaching over 300 feet (91 meters). The tallest known giant sequoia, named "Hyperion", measures around 379.7 feet (115.7 meters).

Weight:

Mature giant sequoias can weigh an astonishing up to 2.7 million pounds (1.2 million kilograms) or more. The largest giant sequoia by volume, "General Sherman", is estimated to weigh around 2.5 million pounds (1.2 million kg).

Root System:

Giant sequoias have a relatively shallow root system for such massive trees. Despite their size, the roots of a giant sequoia typically spread out laterally, covering an area of up to 1 acre (0.4 hectares).

The roots can extend outward up to 100 to 200 feet (30 to 60 meters) from the trunk but rarely grow deeper than 6 to 12 feet (2 to 4 meters) underground.

Unlike some trees with a taproot, giant sequoias rely on their broad and interwoven root systems for stability, with smaller feeder roots helping absorb nutrients and water.

This shallow, wide-spreading root system helps them withstand harsh winds and maintain stability, even in their immense size.

If you can imagine that the family of God is spiritually interwoven among local churches, now around the world, to give us strength to get us through the heavy loads that life sends our way. Standing alone on a tap root is an easy target for Satan to bring down.

7. Purpose and Mission

Shared Purpose in God's Kingdom: God's plan for marriage often includes a shared mission or purpose in advancing His Kingdom. Couples are called to encourage one another in faith and work together for God's glory, whether raising children, serving in ministry, or supporting each other's callings (Genesis 1:28; Matthew 28:19).

8. Patience and Perseverance

Endurance through Trials: James 1:2-4 reminds us that trials build perseverance and maturity. In marriage, difficult times are inevitable, but God's plan includes growing stronger through those challenges by relying on Him and each other.

Patience in Love: 1 Corinthians 13:4-7 describes love as patient and kind, reminding couples to be patient with each other's growth and challenges.

God's plan for a successful marriage is grounded in love, mutual respect, faithfulness, and a shared journey of spiritual growth. When a couple places God at the center of their relationship and follows His guidance, they can experience a deep, lasting, and joyful partnership that reflects His love and grace. Marriage should look like a masterpiece of art. It can be sketchy at first, but as all the corrections are made along the way, it ends in a Masterpiece for God.

To once again, borrow the example of the Kintsugi Art that consists of joining the pieces of objects made of ceramic or other materials, using some adhesive material mixed with gold dust, silver, or other precious material. That way, objects are repaired ostentatiously, in which the importance of the joints or breaks surpasses even that of the original object, which is reborn with a new beauty. This process creates a kind of "golden scar" that highlights the cracks and makes the object even more beautiful and valuable than before.

My loss of Jeannie became my gain to a new, beautiful wife and another BEAUTIFUL spirit that loves walking close to God and leading others to surrender their lives to him. I pray these shared thoughts will be a blessing unto you.

I hope this book helps make everyone's life more beautiful and leads many young couples and seniors into deep, loving relationships so that their spirits mature into a very positive God influence. May you be the gold in healing broken souls by sharing your love and God's stories. Lead your soulmate, family, community, and people around the globe toward the blessing of Jesus and how to live a redeemed and beautiful life.

Fill your life with God's fruits and he will fill your cracks with his golden Love, and his Hands of Love will bless you, so your love and your life will bless others.

Remember your daily mission: it is to rise up each morning with gratitude in your heart, thanking God for the gift of a new day filled with opportunities and potential. As you step into the world, allow yourself to be guided down the path that God has laid out for you, embracing the journey ahead.

Each day presents a chance for you to empty your "Love Basket," which symbolizes the love, kindness, and compassion you can share with others. This act is not merely a personal mission; it has a broader impact on those around you. When you choose to spread love and positivity, you contribute to a ripple effect that can transform your community and beyond.

As we navigate the complexities of our lives, it's essential to recognize how these small acts of kindness can shape the future. In a world increasingly driven by technology, our interactions can sometimes feel impersonal. However, by consciously choosing to engage with others in meaningful ways, we remind ourselves of the human connection that lies at the core of our existence.

So, as you shine His light into the world, remember that your mission is not just about personal fulfillment; it is about harnessing the power of love in a rapidly evolving landscape. The choices you make today, the kindness you extend, and the light you share can have profound implications for how we navigate our interconnected lives tomorrow. Embrace this mission wholeheartedly, knowing that your contributions can help foster a brighter, more compassionate future for all.

Remember, our daily mission is to empty our love basket, which provides the ESSENTIAL nutrient of LOVE to all of God's family, and to the lost of the world. It is my prayer that "The Hands of Love" will bless some soul along their way, I am not sure how many, but God knows.

References

Acts 17:24

The God who made the world and everything in it is the Lord of heaven and earth and does not live in temples built by human hands.

2 Timothy 1:6

Appeal for Loyalty to Paul and the Gospel

For this reason I remind you to fan into flame the gift of God, which is in you through the laying on of my hands.

Matthew 8:3

Jesus reached out his hand and touched the man. "I am willing," he said. "Be clean!" Immediately he was cleansed of his leprosy."

Matthew 8:15

He touched her hand and the fever left her, and she got up and began to wait on him.

Matthew 9:18

Jesus Raises a Dead Girl and Heals a Sick Woman

While he was saying this, a synagogue leader came and knelt before him and said, "My daughter has just died. But come and put your hand on her, and she will live."

Matthew 9:25

After the crowd had been put outside, he went in and took the girl by the hand, and she got up.

Matthew 12:10

And a man with a shriveled hand was there. Looking for a reason to bring charges against Jesus, they asked him, "Is it lawful to heal on the Sabbath?"

Matthew 12:13

Then he said to the man, "Stretch out your hand." So he stretched it out and it was completely restored, just as sound as the other.

Matthew 18:8

If your hand or your foot causes you to stumble, cut it off and throw it away. It is better for you to enter life maimed or crippled than to have two hands or two feet and be thrown into eternal fire.

Mark 14:58

We heard him say, "I will destroy this temple made with human hands and in three days will build another, not made with hands."

Hands in the Bible

- <u>**All (1416)**</u>

<u>**Old Testament (1178)**</u>

- <u>Genesis (46)</u>
- <u>Exodus (88)</u>
- <u>Leviticus (38)</u>
- <u>Numbers (18)</u>
- <u>Deuteronomy (61)</u>
- <u>Joshua (22)</u>
- <u>Judges (67)</u>
- <u>Ruth (3)</u>
- <u>1 Samuel (81)</u>
- <u>2 Samuel (43)</u>
- <u>1 Kings (26)</u>
- <u>2 Kings (33)</u>
- <u>1 Chronicles (28)</u>
- <u>2 Chronicles (39)</u>
- <u>Ezra (14)</u>
- <u>Nehemiah (12)</u>
- <u>Esther (5)</u>
- <u>Job (54)</u>
- <u>Psalm (121)</u>
- <u>Proverbs (30)</u>
- <u>Ecclesiastes (12)</u>
- <u>Song of Songs (4)</u>
- <u>Isaiah (89)</u>
- <u>Jeremiah (79)</u>
- <u>Lamentations (18)</u>
- <u>Ezekiel (90)</u>

- <u>Daniel (17)</u>
- <u>Hosea (5)</u>
- <u>Joel (1)</u>
- <u>Amos (4)</u>
- <u>Obadiah (1)</u>
- <u>Jonah (1)</u>
- <u>Micah (5)</u>
- <u>Nahum (1)</u>
- <u>Habakkuk (2)</u>
- <u>Zephaniah (3)</u>
- <u>Haggai (2)</u>
- <u>Zechariah (11)</u>
- <u>Malachi (4)</u>

<u>New Testament (239)</u>

- <u>Matthew (38)</u>
- <u>Mark (34)</u>
- <u>Luke (36)</u>
- <u>John (17)</u>
- <u>Acts (47)</u>
- <u>Romans (2)</u>
- <u>1 Corinthians (6)</u>
- <u>2 Corinthians (3)</u>
- <u>Galatians (2)</u>
- <u>Ephesians (4)</u>
- <u>Colossians (4)</u>
- <u>1 Thessalonians (1)</u>
- <u>2 Thessalonians (1)</u>
- <u>1 Timothy (4)</u>
- <u>2 Timothy (2)</u>
- <u>Philemon (1)</u>

- <u>Hebrews (11)</u>
- <u>James (1)</u>
- <u>1 Peter (3)</u>
- <u>1 John (1)</u>
- <u>Revelation (21)</u>
- **<u>Hands of Love (1)</u>**